≠
M574d

Other books by Carolyn Meyer

NON-FICTION

AMISH PEOPLE:
Plain Living in a Complex World

THE CENTER:
From a Troubled Past to a New Life

THE MYSTERY OF THE ANCIENT MAYA
(co-authored by Charles Gallenkamp)

ESKIMOS: GROWING UP IN A CHANGING CULTURE

FICTION

C.C. POINDEXTER

EULALIA'S ISLAND

THE SUMMER I LEARNED ABOUT LIFE

THE LUCK OF TEXAS MCCOY

ELLIOTT AND WIN
(Margaret K. McElderry Books)

Denny's Tapes

Denny's Tapes

Carolyn Meyer

Margaret K. McElderry Books
NEW YORK

"When Sue Wears Red" and "Ardella" copyright © 1926 and renewed
1954 by Langston Hughes. Reprinted from SELECTED POEMS OF
LANGSTON HUGHES by permission of Alfred A. Knopf, Inc.

"Ol' Man River" written by Oscar Hammerstein II & Jerome Kern
Copyright © 1927 T.B. Harms Company. Copyright Renewed.
(c/o The Welk Music Group, Santa Monica California, 90401).
International Copyright Secured. All Rights Reserved. Used by Permission.

Margaret K. McElderry Books
Macmillan Publishing Company
866 Third Avenue
New York, NY 10022
Collier Macmillan Canada, Inc.

First Edition
Printed in the United States of America
10   9   8   7   6   5   4   3   2   1

Composition by Maryland Linotype Composition Company
Baltimore, Maryland
Printed and bound by Fairfield Graphics
Fairfield, Pennsylvania
Designed by Barbara A. Fitzsimmons

Library of Congress Cataloging-in-Publication Data

Meyer, Carolyn.
Denny's tapes.

Summary: When seventeen-year-old Denny, who is
black, falls in love with his white stepsister and
her father throws him out, he drives cross-country
to find his own father, whom he barely knows.
{1. Afro-Americans—Fiction.   2. Stepchildren—
Fiction}   I. Title.
PZ7.M5685Ph   1987   {Fic}   87–4038
ISBN 0–689–50413–6

To
Joan,
Ron,
and
Terry

Tape 1

This is the voice of Denny Brown, Friday, June 27th, somewhere in Pennsylvania.

I wish I'd had a chance to say good-bye to Stephanie. I didn't. It was a case of grab some clothes, collect some money, and _go_.

Would Stephanie have come with me, if I'd asked her? Probably not. She has a lot of guts, but not for running away. She's a rebel, but she's not crazy, not a nut case. Hang around with me awhile and she might be, though. Steffy has a future without me, and the question right now is if I have any future at all. This is the time to find out.

So I am now on Interstate 80 in my trusty rusty Plymouth named Mary, headed west with four hundred thirty-seven dollars, last week's pay plus what's left of my life savings, to get me to the other side of the country. I can sell this tape recorder, graduation present from my mother, worth maybe a hundred, if it gets down to that.

Meanwhile I have a stack of blank tapes, and I'll talk to the machine, which is like talking to yourself, while I drive across the U.S., away from one crazy family and maybe toward another one. I've got a lot to find out.

Well. My name is Dennis James Brown, Denny to my friends, and I am seventeen years old—eighteen next month—and a high school graduate as of three weeks ago. My problem, Doctor Panasonic, is that I am in love with Stephanie West, a beautiful girl with a great future as a dancer. Stephanie West is the daughter of Grant West, my mother's present husband.

Rule One: Never fall in love with your stepsister.

Rule Two: If you do, be very careful not to let your stepfather find out, or he is likely to kick your ass. He may also scream something like, "Get out of here, you black bastard, and don't ever show your face around here again."

That is not totally accurate. I am not a bastard, but I am black. Or half black, I'd rather say, but I'm learning there is no such thing. My mother, Lucy Sunderland Brown West, is white. My father, James Dennis Brown, is black. That makes me half and half, coffee with cream or cream with coffee, depending on your point of view. The black part lives in San Francisco, the spot on the map at the other end of I-80.

At least he did at one time, and that is where I am headed now, trusting my luck to Mary, eleven years old, 110,462 miles. I bought her six months ago with the money I earned at Gochnaur's Pennsylvania Dutch Woodcrafters. Mary is the reason I have so little cash. Now we will see if taking Mary apart every weekend since April, replacing her vital organs one at a time, has put her in good enough shape to get me where I am going.

I really wanted to punch Grant West in the face. *Doctor* Grant West. Grant always makes sure you remember he's a doctor. Punch him not for the name he called me, but for what calling me that must have done to my mother. For the past seventeen years my mother has been trying to protect me from cruelty. The worst cruelties happen in your own family. They say most murders are committed by a relative, someone close to you, not some stranger on the street who doesn't like your looks.

Mother thought if she brought me up white, then everybody would treat me white. But I saw in that one instant—"you black bastard"—that it was a fantasy, fragile as glass. The fantasy shattered into a million pieces because I love Grant's daughter, and he's scared out of his mind that I might have touched her and spoiled her precious Whiteness. In his flash of rage I saw that Grant had married Mother even though *her* precious Whiteness had been spoiled by James Dennis Brown. I wonder if Mother saw that, too.

So here I am roaring over the roller-coaster hills of western Pennsylvania, stopping once in a while to take a leak and get some coffee. Right away I began thinking of things I wish I had with me, like Grant's stainless-steel Thermos. Mostly, though, I wish I had Stephanie.

Funny how you can know somebody for years and years

and nothing happens, and then all of a sudden, *WHAM*, it hits you like an earthquake. Stephanie and I met when I was seven and she was six and our parents made the fatal move of marrying each other. Fatal for us; I don't know about them. I can't figure how Mother puts up with him, but then I guess she isn't so easy either. Steffy and I hated each other for most of the past eleven years. She was a spoiled little brat, a princess. Her father even called her Princess. When she was six she would run to him like a two-year-old with her arms up. "Pick me up, Daddy!" He'd carry her around as though she were a baby, and she'd look down at me and stick her tongue out. Made me sick.

Princess Stephanie lived in Philadelphia in a castle with her mother and her rich grandparents. In the beginning Stephanie came to see her father on certain holidays and half the summer. I did not look forward to those visits. She ran around dressed up in a pink tutu with pink tights and little pink slippers with ribbons tied around her ankles. She'd twirl and strike poses, holding her arms this way and that way, one leg stuck out behind her or bent up in front of her. One year she couldn't come at Christmas until after she had danced in *The Nutcracker*. Grant went all the way to Philadelphia just to see her in that show.

When Steffy was ten and I was eleven, Corky was born. Imagine naming a kid Cochran West. That was Grant's mother's name, Cochran. You can't even tell from the name if it's a boy or a girl. We think Corky is turning out to be a girl, but she has a ways to go.

At first Stephanie tried to play mommy to this screaming,

purple-faced infant, and that only made the kid scream harder. Mother kept saying, "Dear, please don't love her so *hard.*" She never had to say that to me, because I just ignored little Cochran West. Babies weren't something I was interested in when I was eleven. I had enough other problems, the biggest of which was school. I was not doing very well at school. Actually I was doing well enough to please myself but not anybody else.

Mother likes to tell about when we first moved to Vicksburg and I was ready to start school. They tested me and decided I was bright and put me in a special program for gifted children. It seemed like just so much b.s. to me. I don't actually remember saying, "It's too much work—why bother?" but that's how I felt, and that's what Mother told everybody I said, making a joke out of it to get over the embarrassment of having her gifted child thrown out of the gifted program in the third month. By the time I got to middle school, nobody remembered that I was a gifted child. I just barely got by. The only class I really liked was music, but when Mother rented a piano and signed me up for music lessons, I never practiced. "The trouble with Denny is he has no discipline," everybody said. I had it for what I liked—when I first started working I bought myself a little electronic keyboard, and I loved to fool around with that.

Last fall there was a major blowup in the Philadelphia castle, something to do with a guy named Bart Schwartz. Grant took off for Philly and came back with Stephanie and a ton of luggage.

All that time when she wasn't around much, Steffy was turning beautiful and I hadn't noticed. I was too worried about my pimples and other signs of male development, more into playing soccer, hanging out with the guys, sneaking into movies, stuff like that. When Stephanie came to live with us and I realized the caterpillar had turned into a butterfly, I was so self-conscious I could hardly look at her, and at the same time I didn't want to do anything *but* look at her. Talk about embarrassing. Whenever she was in the house I was miserable, because when I did look at her I thought about . . . things.

For the first couple of weeks after she moved to the Burg she hardly ever came out of her room. She refused to go to school. She looked pale and puffy-eyed, as though she had been crying. She wore nothing but black—black skirts and pants, black shirts and sweaters—and no lipstick. She started wearing her thick glasses again instead of her contact lenses. Nobody wanted to notice that she just moved the food around on her plate—nobody but Corky, who has a habit of calling attention to things other people are trying to ignore.

"Is she always going to look this weird?" Corky demanded. "And how come she doesn't eat anything?"

Grant laid down his knife and fork and stared at Stephanie, who stared sullenly at her plate. "No," he said, "she is not. And starting tomorrow morning, she's going to school."

That meant I got conned into being her escort and showing her where everything was, this white-faced, thin-as-a-stick girl, who dressed like a widow, had a splayed-out dancer's walk, and always seemed to be staring off into space. The girls of the Burg were not likely to go for this, and the guys didn't know what to think. I decided to hell with it, she wasn't my problem.

That night after dinner, while I was listening to some old jazz records, she glided silently into my room and folded down on the floor, where she crouched like a spider. I didn't know *what* to do, so I didn't do anything or say anything, just kept spinning disks. Next night she came back. Then it got to be a habit. Every evening after dinner, I'd be listening to jazz—Duke Ellington, Louis Armstrong, Dizzy Gillespie—and she'd come and sit on the floor and listen with me.

"Makes you want to dance, doesn't it?" I said.

"Go ahead," she said with a shrug, as though dancing didn't make the least bit of difference in her life.

"I don't dance," I said. "But listen to this."

I tried a little improvising on the keyboard, a Duke Ellington tune, just fooling around. She actually smiled, and her eyes looked alive behind the huge glasses for the first time since she'd come there.

With an audience like Stephanie, I worked harder. I'd wait till she'd go back downstairs to her own room, and then I'd work on a few more tunes to play for her. And we started talking about music.

One evening at dinner when nobody was paying attention, I whispered, "Eat everything on your plate or I won't play for you." She shot me a hateful look and stalked away from the table, nose in the air. I wanted to yell after her, hey, it's okay, only kidding—but I didn't.

For a couple of nights she didn't come around, and I felt terrible. Then one night she was back. I was glad to see her, but I said, "No eating, no playing."

She gave me that same haughty look. "Okay," she said finally. "Let's go see what's in the kitchen."

So we crept downstairs and poked through the refrigerator until she found a few things she considered worthy of consumption. It wasn't much, but at least she ate. And then we went back up to my room and I played. After about a week of that I said, "Listen, wouldn't it be easier if you just ate the regular meal with the rest of us?" She shrugged and said, "Yeah, I guess so," and that was it.

Stephanie will never be fat, but pretty soon she lost that hollow look, as though all the marrow had drained out of her bones. She started wearing contact lenses again. And I kept playing for her, little tunes I made up.

We started talking more. I told her about my dad, what I knew about him, which wasn't actually that much. "Don't you wonder about him?" she asked me.

"Sometimes." He faded out of the picture when Grant faded in. I hadn't seen him in several years—just a few postcards and a couple of letters.

"If I were you I'd want to find him," she said.

"You're not me."

"Thank goodness," she said with a funny little giggle, "or I wouldn't be able to do this."

She leaned over and put her arms around me and kissed

me, full on the mouth, long and slow. And my world has been spinning ever since, but not the same direction the rest of the world spins.

Crossed the Pennsylvania-Ohio border this afternoon, June 27th, at 3:25 p.m.

Last night after Grant threw me out, I drove down to the river and slept in my car. "Slept" is a gross exaggeration. I dozed a little and thought a lot. About four-thirty, before anybody was awake, I went back and got my camping gear out of the storage room above the garage. I loaded Mary and drove out to the furniture shop and dozed some more. Gochy came in about six, his usual time.

"I'm sorry," I said. "I know this is real short notice, but I'm in a ton of trouble at home, and I'm going away for a while until it blows over."

"Bad time for you to leave," he said. "Got a lot of work now."

"I know. I'm sorry."

"When you coming back, Denny?"

"I don't know," I said. The truth was, maybe never.

Gochy is a fusty old Pennsylvania Dutchman who looks like one of the Seven Dwarfs and runs a woodshop in an old barn behind his house. He makes copies of antiques: rocking chairs and deacon's benches and harvest tables and something he calls a "dry sink." I think everybody on our street has one of those dry sinks. They use them for liquor cabinets. I did most of the finishing, and he promised to teach me to do some joining.

It wasn't a bad job, and Gochy's wife used to come by with things for me to eat, molasses cookies and sugar pies and so on. I liked Aunt Kissy—that's what he calls her—until the day I went to the back of the shop for something and heard her say to him, "Where's the nigger?" And heard him shush her. It was bound to happen, but it was worse because I thought she was my friend. After that I wouldn't eat any of her damn pies or cookies, no matter how good they looked.

Gochy paid me off from a stash he keeps hidden someplace and said, "Good luck, Denny. See you when you get back," and I said, "Thanks." I hid the roll of bills in my sleeping bag, which nobody in his right mind would want to steal, it's that funky. Then I filled the gas tank and sat around waiting for the bank to open. I stood in line waiting to withdraw my money, as nervous as if I was robbing the place. One thing about having my whole life blow up in my face on a Thursday was that the banks were open and I could collect my cash. By the time all that was done, it was safe to go back to the house.

Grant, of course, was already at the hospital, doing rounds. He's a cardiologist. I hope nothing is ever wrong with my heart and I have to go to somebody like him. Mother was down at the high school, teaching a special French summer course. I wished that Stephanie would be there, but she wasn't. I didn't really think she would be. After what happened the night before, Grant would have her practically locked up. Stephanie is working this summer in Grant's office, as a receptionist.

The one I had to watch out for was Corky. Corky is six and always hanging around. She's a supergenius who plans to become a famous scientist when she grows up. One day it's a microbiologist and the next day an experimental physicist, but always famous. She expects a Nobel Prize. She'll probably get it. Corky was supposed to be a couple of blocks away at a sitter's, but she is always escaping from the sitter's and coming home to work on her experiments. Grant bought himself a computer, and Corky is the one who knows how to use it. Not on dumb games, either. The point here is that if Corky had gotten away from Shirley again, I would have a hard time getting what I needed: the clothes from my room on the third floor, my tape recorder, and my mother's address book.

There was no sign of Corky, and collecting my stuff was simple. But I could not find the address book. How many places could there be to put it? It should have been in a desk drawer, in handy reach, near the telephone in the room she calls her study. Mother has an antique rolltop desk with all kinds of drawers and slots and cubbyholes. But my mother is not an organized person, and the book wasn't in any of the places I thought it might be. There was nothing to do but sit down and go through each drawer and slot and cubbyhole methodically. It would have helped if my hands weren't sweating so much.

I was about to give up when I happened to glance on the shelf where she keeps her cookbooks—she does not keep them in the kitchen—and there it was. In it were the three addresses I needed.

The first was James Dennis Brown. His address had been changed so many times, crossed out and erased and written over, I could hardly read it. I wasn't sure which was the most recent, but the address I could make out best was in Berkeley, California.

The second one was Eugenia Brown, my grandmother. She lives in Chicago, and it looked as though she never moved.

The third was Grace Sunderland in Nebraska, my other grandmother. There was only one change for her.

I copied them on a file card.

"What are you doing, Denny?"

There was Corky. In a minute the phone would ring, and it would be Shirley, her sitter, who was not the most energetic person or the smartest, calling to say, "Corky? You come on back down here now."

Meanwhile, though, Corky was standing in the doorway to my mother's study, staring at me. Any fool could see I had been going through her desk. "Looking for . . . uh . . . a dictionary."

"Yeah? What are you going to look up?"

I tried to think of a word she wouldn't know, but she probably knows as many as I do.

"None of your business," I said, always the last resort in dealing with snoopy little sisters.

"How come you're not at work?"

"Gochy sent me to borrow a dictionary so he could look up some words." I have never been a good liar, and this lie fascinated her.

"*Gochy* wants to look up some words? I bet you I know any word Gochy knows. And how come he needs to know weird words anyway?"

"You're probably right, Corky. Now I gotta get back to work."

The phone rang. That would be Shirley. "Me, too," Corky said. She thought she was taking care of Shirley, not the other way around. She was probably right about that, too.

"Be good, Corky," I said. "Take care of things."

I wrote a note for Mother: "Gone camping. Love, Denny." And another one for Steffy: "I love you."

I thought about stopping by Grant's office to say good-bye to Stephanie, but that would be asking for trouble. One look at her and I wouldn't want to leave. But I had to. I knew that. Someday I'd see her again, when I got it all straightened out.

There was a picture of her on Grant's dresser, a school photo in a silver frame. I slipped the picture out and left the frame. I thought of putting a picture of me in its place. That would have frosted him good. I propped the note on Stephanie's desk and looked around her room one more time, and then I left.

I wasn't on the road long before I realized I hadn't eaten anything. I stopped for a couple of burgers and fries, and when I paid for them, I thought, No, Denny, you can't live this way. After today, when there's some space between me and the West family, then I'll stop and cook a meal on the Coleman stove and figure out what I'm going to do when I get to Chicago. I figure I have to stay out of sight until July 29th, when I turn eighteen, and then they won't be able to come after me. Of course, there is always the possibility they aren't coming after me now. If it's up to Grant, they won't. But Mother would. I'm betting he'll talk her out of it.

Five a.m. Saturday, June 28th. Ohio, somewhere.

It's raining. My tent started to leak, and my sleeping bag soaked up some water. Now I am jammed in Mary's front seat with my soggy Northland for company.

Once I crossed the border into Ohio yesterday I got a whole different feeling about what I was doing. There was no going back, even though I had clicked off only 232 miles, and if I had turned around I could have been home by dark. But that isn't home anymore, and I was too tired to drive much farther without some sleep, even though it was only four o'clock.

I wondered if Corky had told anybody, or Mother had spotted my note on her messy desk, or Grant had discovered that Stephanie's picture was missing—but not Stephanie. I tried not to wonder what she was doing, but it was impossible not to think about Steffy, her skin, her hair—well.

At a rest stop I studied the map for tiny red trees that mean camping areas. I-80 is a toll road through Ohio, loaded with eighteen-wheelers that almost swallow Mary when they roar by. I wanted to get off the road for a while.

I finally found a campground that didn't charge eight dollars for a family of four, even if there was only one person. But the ground was all chewed up with ruts, and there was hardly any place you'd really want to pitch a tent. I didn't care. I bought a quart of milk, a couple cans of beans, a loaf of bread, and some lunch meat at the camp store. Then I found out I had left my cooking kit behind, but at least I had a can opener in the glove compartment. I sat at a splintery picnic table and ate the beans cold, straight from the can, plus a couple of sandwiches, and washed them down with milk, watching the sun go down, thinking things over. Then I crawled inside my sleeping bag and thought some more.

To go back to the beginning: My mother, Lucy Sunderland, grew up on a farm in Nebraska, one of the places I intend to stop. All she wanted to do when she was a kid was to get away from the corn and wheat fields. Her dream was to live in Paris. She went to college and studied French. Somehow she got the idea that she was the reincarnation of a French writer named George Sand, a weird lady who went by a man's name and smoked cigars and wore pants in Paris long before anybody else did. This woman named George Sand died on June 8, 1876. June 8th is my mother's birthday, and that coincidence proved her reincarnation theory. After college she got a scholarship to go to Paris to study more French and more about this woman who smoked cigars.

Mother was sitting at a sidewalk cafe, she told me, and she heard somebody at a table behind her speaking to the waiter in terrible French with an American accent. She turned around, and there was a big tall black guy with incredible green eyes. They started talking, back and forth, and then he came and sat with her, and they drank cheap wine and talked half the night. She said it felt as though they had been friends for years and years.

James Dennis Brown was not a hippie, she says, but a musician who got sick of the way America treats its black people, and he decided to hang out in Paris for a while. He got some gigs playing piano in little clubs, making barely enough to survive. Then along came my mother, and *BOOM*, lightning flashes, stars exploding, magic. She said they talked once in a while about how it was okay in Paris, but if they ever went back to America they'd have a tough time of it, being an interracial couple. "But we were crazy in love with each other," she said. "You don't think too clearly when you're crazy in love." I learned that myself, on my own.

They hung out in Paris for a couple of years. She found out all she ever wanted to know about George Sand, enough to write her dissertation for her Ph.D., and he had some good gigs, and they had a great time together. Then she found out she was going to have a baby, and he said it's going to be trouble, and she said I don't care. He said okay, so they got married and decided to come back to the U.S. to have the baby—me—and make peace with their families.

That's when the tomatoes hit the fan. Mother had always been the darling of her family, the one who got all the honors and prizes at school, Daddy's little girl who could do no wrong. She and my dad checked into a motel in

Ogallala—she did the checking in for both of them—and she went out to the farm by herself to break the news gently, so that Dad could come over later to meet them and not be a shock, you know, walking up to the front door in all his six feet four of blackness.

But Grandma fainted and Grandpa just stared at her when she told them, punching his fist into his hand and not saying anything, until Lucy got up and walked out. She left the name of the motel, in case they wanted to call her. Two days went by and there was no call, so Lucy tried one more time and phoned them. Grandma was crying so hard she couldn't talk, and Grandpa took the phone out of her hands and said, "Don't never come back here while you're married to a nigger."

So she didn't. Their next stop was Chicago, where Dad's family lives. The reception there wasn't a whole lot better, but not for the same reasons you'd expect. The Browns are upper-class blacks, Mother says, and they thought my dad had thrown away a good education and a lot of talent by going to Paris. Marrying a white girl who came from a bunch of redneck farmers didn't help his reputation any with his family. So they were very polite but *icy*, she said, and she and Dad got out of there and went back to New York.

I was born in New York. They found a little apartment on the West Side, which was run down and miserable then, and Dad went to work in a department store during the day, at Macy's in housewares, because he couldn't support a wife and a baby on whatever he could make playing jazz at night. Mother stayed home with me and got some jobs translating French and tutoring, but it's probably hard to live like that when you think you're the reincarnation of a crazy French writer. They were always broke. Not having money is okay when you're young and carefree in Paris, Mother says, but it's not okay when you're trying to survive in New York with a little kid.

They fought. I remember some of that; nothing specific, just a shred of memory of waking up at night and hearing people yelling at each other. Finally they decided to call it quits, and Dad left. "You can't blame him for leaving," Mother told me. "It wasn't a good life at all."

He promised to send her money every month, and he said he wouldn't come back to see me unless she asked him to. Sometimes the checks came, sometimes they didn't. I guess he did the best he could. Postmarks changed, the banks got farther away. He had been around San Francisco for the last couple of years. We moved a few times. He sent me cards on my birthday and letters at Christmas. I never answered them. I don't know why I didn't. I hardly remember him. But now I'm going all the way out there to see him.

Dr. Grant West is another story. After my dad left, Mother decided she had had enough of city life. She thought it would be good for me to grow up in a nice quiet little town someplace where there was no such thing as racial prejudice. Since she had promised Grandma and Grandpa Sunderland she'd come back as soon as she was rid of "the nigger," she packed up and we went all the way to Nebraska on the bus. Grandpa had died in the meantime, and I guess Mother wanted to make peace. I don't remember much about the visit; probably just as well. Mother said Grandma started to cry every time she looked at me. "I don't suppose he can pass for Greek with that nose?" she wanted to know.

On the way back to New York on the bus, we stopped off at some little town in Pennsylvania. It was green and pretty, a college town, which Mother thought would be more sophisticated and not have so much racial prejudice as New York. She liked the main street and said, "Why not?" Mother is the kind who often says, "Why not?" and goes ahead and does something she regrets later. So that was how we ended up in Vicksburg.

She found a tiny house for us down near the river, which floods sometimes in the spring so that everybody has to be evacuated, and she got a job teaching French at a high school a few miles down the river. They wouldn't hire her at the college because she had never quite finished her dissertation on George Sand for her Ph.D. I was three years old when we moved there.

The rain is still pouring down. It's a sea of mud out there, and Mary is my lifeboat. My mother used to sing me a song in French about a little boat. "*Le petit bateau . . . le petit bateau qui va . . .*" I can't remember the rest. She hasn't been to France since she and my father left, but she talks a lot about going. Or she used to, before Grant. She is a woman who wants to recapture the past. She remembers her romantic student life in Paris twenty years ago. Since then nothing has ever been so carefree. She used to tell me when I was little that she and I were going back there, to make sure I was bilingual, and we'd live part of the time in Paris and part of the time out in the country, where George Sand, her heroine, used to live.

Mother had the idea that when her life settled down she was going to write a novel about being the reincarnation of George Sand. She was going to call it *George Sand and the Katzenjammer Kid*, and it was going to be autobiographical but also literary. There used to be a comic strip about a couple of little Germans who were always raising hell, called "The Katzenjammer Kids." She says her father used to call her Katzenjammer, which if you look it up in the dictionary means, "a hangover," or "distress, depression," or "a discordant clamor." She thought that applied to her.

Mother's life never seemed to settle down. One spring when we were living in our little old house, the river rose and somebody came and told us we had to get out, because it was going to overflow. Mother didn't want to go, but she didn't want to float away, either. We grabbed a few things and stayed with some of her friends until the floodwaters went down. When we went back, the house was full of mud, a total mess. "It's a symbol of my life," she said. But then she cleaned it up and we moved in again.

When I was six years old and ready to start school, I didn't know about being black. She never talked about it. But the other kids seemed to know, and this was a different story.

"Hey, nigger," said this one jerk with the mental capacity of a lima bean. Pretty soon he had a whole gang gathered around us, spitting on the ground and yelling, "Nigger." I knew what they meant. I looked at their faces and went crazy and started pasting into whoever came within reach of my fists. Then everybody was into it, and there was yelling and screaming and bloody noses. Pretty soon a couple of teachers waded in and pulled us apart, and I got marched off to the principal's office and had to sit there for a half hour every afternoon for weeks. The lima bean got off with a talking-to. Everybody agreed I started it.

At home things were in an uproar, too, because Mother had met a doctor who lived a couple of blocks away, and she was busy falling in love. That of course was none other than our Dr. Grant West, whose wife had divorced him and taken their little girl, Stephanie, back to live with her parents in Philadelphia. I had my own problems and didn't pay much attention to what was going on there, except that one day Mother sat me down and said they were getting married.

"I need a man in my life," she explained, as though that explained anything. "I'm not the kind of woman who can make it by myself."

"You have me," I said, stupid little kid.

She said, "Yes, I know that, and I love you. But I'm going to marry Grant. For both of us."

She explained that we were very, very lucky, because not every man in the world is able to accept a woman and her child if that child happens to be "different." It took me a while to figure out what she meant by that.

So there was a wedding in the college chapel and everybody went down to the Vicksburg Inn for a reception afterward, including this kid, Stephanie, who came all the way up from Philadelphia for the occasion. There was a lot of picture-taking that day, and even some of Stephanie and me holding hands, which everybody thought was cute. Dr. West's brother and his parents were there, and they fussed over me as though I were a pet ferret or something, but I overheard some remarks made about how Grant had always been so broad-minded and so on, and he didn't know what he was getting into, taking on somebody else's child, which is always difficult, and in a case like this, why there's just no end to the things that could happen. . . .

It wasn't for both of us that she married him, I knew right then. It was for her.

Mother and I moved out of our cozy place on Water Street, where I could lie in bed and look out my little window and watch the river flowing majestically by, and into the doctor's huge old house on Third Street with a historical plaque on it. I had the attic room on the top floor, and although I couldn't see the river, I could look into the bedroom window of the people across the street, which was sometimes fairly entertaining. I liked it because it was so big. It was easy to go off and be by myself. But not as easy as I thought, or Grant would not have walked in on us two nights ago.

I learned to stay out of Grant's way. He was all right, I

guess. Life drifted along like our big river for several years, with two major changes. One was that the king and queen had a new baby princess named Cochran, whom I nicknamed Corky. The other was that last September, at the beginning of my senior year, Princess Stephanie had a huge fight with her mother in Philadelphia and came to live with us. I thought she was a royal pain.

I wish I still felt that way. Life would be much easier. The night before last, Steffy was lying on my bed when her father walked in and found us wrapped in each other's arms. Grant hardly ever came up to my room, but that night he did—I forget why. Now the thing is, we hadn't actually *done* anything, although I will admit that in another ten minutes, or maybe five, we probably would have. We had been talking about it for a long time, about what it would mean in our lives. And we were in love. . . .

I did not plan on falling in love with Grant West's daughter. It was probably the biggest mistake I ever made in my life, but I don't know how to turn that around, to run the film backward. I don't think I'd erase it even if I knew how. The fact is, I am bogged down in a muddy campground in Ohio, and Steffy is a prisonor in Vicksburg, Pennsylvania, and it's my fault. I dream of ways to rescue her, of swooping through the Burg and carrying her off like a knight on a horse, but that's only a dream. The fact is that Stephanie is going to have to rescue herself.

Tape 2

Sunday, June 29th. Indiana. More rain. The windshield wipers are not keeping up with it too well. The only thing dry is the cereal I ate for breakfast. Now I'm on the road again, thinking ahead to Chicago and finding my grandmother, Eugenia Brown. My grandfather's name was Ulysses Brown, but he died when I was about seven.

I have a lot of cousins out there somewhere. My father has four brothers, and if each one has only two kids, then I've got eight cousins. I don't know their names, but I plan to look them up when I get to Chicago.

Besides the worn-out windshield wipers, I keep hearing a weird noise coming from somewhere in the car, a kind of *klunk . . . klunk*, which I am pretending is my imagination. When certain things go wrong, you pretend you're imagining them. Your tongue is not feeling a hole in your tooth, and that tooth does not hurt when you eat ice cream. Your car is not making a strange noise, because it can't, dammit, it just can't! But there it is: *klunk . . . klunk*.

Oh, Stephanie, what are you doing now?

The time zone has changed, so I reset my watch and Mary's clock. It's an hour earlier here than it is at 212 Third Street. Mother is in class. Corky has gotten away from Shirley and is making some kind of strange mess in the kitchen. Stephanie is at Grant's office, answering the phone: "Dr. West's office. May I help you?" Yes, you can, Stephanie. Maybe I could call her at the office and say, "Stephanie, I love you." It would be worth it if she says, "Denny, I love you, too." But what is either one of us going to do about it? She is guarded by a dragon. Her mother is a dragon, too, she says.

Steffy came to live with us because her mother wouldn't let her date a Jewish guy named Bart Schwartz. Her mother is prejudiced against Jews. Bart is at Princeton and intends to go to Yale Law School and then to become a Rhodes scholar and study at Oxford in England and to practice international law. When Steffy's mother refused to let her see him anymore, Steffy defied her and sneaked up to Princeton for a weekend, and the roof blew off. That's when Grant brought her to the Burg. Grant calls him "an arrogant young snot," which is *not* the same as being a black bastard, and he's probably wished a thousand times since then he had urged her to run away with the future international lawyer. Being Jewish doesn't compare at all with being black; it's a hundred times better.

Stephanie calls her mother "The Archduchess of the City of Brotherly Love." Philadelphia means "brotherly love" in Greek, which was probably William Penn's idea of a good joke. One night when Steffy and I had been kissing each other for hours and driving each other crazy, she pulled away and looked at me and said, "Is this what they mean by brotherly love? What do you suppose *sisterly* love is like?" After that, our code word for wanting to make out was "Philadelphia!"

Of course we're not really brother and sister, we're no blood relation at all, but we both knew we'd be in deep trouble if our parents found out about us. I never wanted to be an actor or thought I had any talent at all along those lines, but Steffy and I kept up a performance as though we could hardly stand each other. We got so good at putting each other down in front of our parents that sometimes we'd have to find a chance to say, "Hey, listen, this is all part of the act, right?" I wondered what would happen if we ever had a real fight.

We didn't, though. I think everything about Stephanie is the way it ought to be, and she thinks the same about me. The thing we don't agree on is the future. Stephanie is a very determined girl. She says she's a dancer, that dancers dance, and that's the way it has to be. She says she knows how hard it is to break in, how hard she'll have to work, and all the sacifices she'll have to make to reach her goal.

"What about me?" I'd ask her, and she'd say, "Well, Denny, what *about* you?" And I never knew how to answer. Here I am, out of high school without the least idea about what I'm going to do next. Gochy wants me to work with him in his woodshop, specializing in fake antiques. He's taught me a lot about tools and about wood, so I have a real respect for them. He has a brother who is a blacksmith, and the brother said if I ever got tired of wood and wanted to learn iron, he'd teach me. Not shoeing horses but making fireplace tools and hinges, which Gochy sometimes puts on his fake antiques. But I can't see myself doing that for very long. I don't want to live in the Burg, for one thing. Unlike Bart Schwartz, eighteen and already an international lawyer in his head, I have no idea what I want.

Mother has tried to talk to me about it. "We can work out the money for college," she says. "All you have to do is decide what you want."

All you have to do is go over Niagara Falls in a barrel. All you have to do is perform brain surgery on your own head. I don't know, and it often makes me mad at Stephanie, because she knows exactly what she wants, and it is not easy to be around someone who is that focused.

"You're like a laser beam," I tell her.

I'd be sitting on the floor of her bedroom, which she turned into a dance studio. After Grant brought her back from the lair of the Philadelphia dragon, and she got over her depression and started eating and listening to jazz with me, she talked Grant into installing mirrors and a ballet *barre* along one wall of her room. She has a narrow single bed, more like a cot, and two huge dressers, and a closet stuffed with more clothes than any person could possibly keep track of—racks of shoes, all kinds of stuff, kept in perfect order. You'd expect someone like Stephanie to be messy, clothes dropped wherever she takes them off, but she says that's part of discipline. Corky is like that, too. It must be their father's genes. Corky's room looks like a science lab, and she's not the least bit interested in clothes. Sort of like my mother, who can wear the same clothes and eat the same food for ten days straight, unless somebody reminds her to change or to cook something different.

I did not inherit genes for goals, apparently. Mother might have started out knowing what she wanted, to be another George Sand, but she got sidetracked. I don't know what my father wanted, except to play music. I don't even know what he got. Which is why I decided I have to find out who *he* is if I'm ever going to figure out who *I* am, and who I am going to be.

I drive along the highway, windshield wipers clacking back and forth, back and forth, and I picture Stephanie at the *barre*, every muscle taut. Stephanie cross-legged on her narrow bed, brushing her long dark hair. Stephanie running down the hall wrapped in a towel, another towel tied like a turban around her head. Stephanie bright and cheerful at breakfast but dopey at night. (I am just the opposite. Mother told me my dad could stay up all night, but don't try to hold a conversation with him before noon; in that respect I am like my father.) Stephanie in tights, Stephanie in baggy jeans, Stephanie in a fuzzy pink sweater; she has very small breasts—she calls them "dancer's tits." Stephanie at the pool in a purple bikini, Stephanie in a flannel nightgown with little red flowers. Stephanie crying because her father yelled at her, Stephanie playing with our sister, Corky. She is part of my family and part of my life, which is both why I am in love with her and why I should not be.

"What's going to happen if the folks find out?" Stephanie asked one day in the spring, when we had gone for a walk down along the river.

"Find out what?"

"About us, of course. What else would I be worried about?"

I had been trying not to think about that. "How are they going to find out? We're being careful."

"It's going to get harder."

She was right. It got a lot harder at the end of the year, when there were graduation parties and dances, and neither of us wanted to go with other people. We wanted to go with each other, and that was impossible.

Once I asked Steffy what she thought about me being black. I was the first black person she ever knew personally, except for her grandparents' maid and gardener. There are lots of blacks in Philadelphia.

"I don't care what color you are," Stephanie said. "I don't care if you're green or purple. I love *you*."

"But that's part of who I am."

"Okay," she said. We were sitting on a rock on the riverbank where nobody could see us, unless they went by in a boat. "Okay, Denny, then who are you?"

"Another part of who I am is that I don't *know* who I am. I'm Dennis Brown, I'm six feet one and a half, which means everybody thinks I should play basketball but I don't, I weigh one sixty, I have skin that looks like a year-round tan, features described as negroid, kinky hair, and green eyes. Grandma Sunderland wishes I could pass for Greek."

"I love your eyes."

"What about the rest? What about the nose? Maybe I could get a cute nose like Michael Jackson's."

"Don't be silly," she said. "You're wonderful-looking. All the girls in school go crazy over you. They think you're absolutely gorgeous."

"They do? I never noticed."

A lie. I know a lot of girls, and I know they like me. I used to take them out. They'd drag me home to meet their parents, and I'd see the look of surprise when Mr. and Mrs. Liberal realized their daughter had brought home a black boyfriend. And they'd be *super*polite, falling all over themselves to be nice to show what great liberals they were. But somewhere down the road the girl would eventually say, "Gee, I guess I'd better not go out with you for a while. My parents don't want me to have a steady boyfriend." And a short time after that, the girl would be hanging out every day at some other guy's locker. Some *white* guy's locker. It doesn't have to happen too often until you get the idea. So I figured, forget it, I'll wait till I get out of the Burg. I told myself it wasn't important, even though it was. Maybe it would always be like this.

I was considered sort of exotic, like the son of the Korean math professor at the college and the girl from India whose father was a visiting scholar teaching a course in

Eastern religions. But I was also considered more dangerous. That Indian girl was generally kept under lock and key by her parents, but once she stood up in class to give a report and talked about arranged marriages in India, and how when her family went back to Bombay, a suitable husband would be found for her. A lot of kids went wild over that idea, asking how she could let such a thing happen, and if she didn't want to run away so that she could be free to fall in love and find her own husband. She just said, "No, it is much better our way." She could be right.

Since girls were such a problem—if not the girls, then their parents—I usually hung out with a bunch of guys. Five of them have a band, and we'd get together in Keith Briggs's basement and jam until all hours. Sometimes I'd sit in with them on drums, but what I enjoyed most was piano. I can play by ear, and I like to improvise, picking out a melody line and putting it with some chords, the way I did with my keyboard at home. They're into rock, though, and I'm more interested in jazz. I wish I had remembered to bring that keyboard with me.

A lot of partying goes on in that town, with a lot of beer. Girls always came around to listen to us jam. It was no big deal. It's a small town, and everybody knows everybody, and on weekends we always partied at somebody's house. Not at mine, though; Grant doesn't like it.

Then Stephanie came to live with us. At first she didn't have anything to do with those parties, where everybody was into drinking beer and getting stupid, but pretty soon she started hanging out with a couple of the girls and showing up with them. I hated that, hated having her there and seeing how the guys looked at her. Because Stephanie is so beautiful. One of them made some crude remarks about her, how convenient for me to have a sweet piece like that living in the same house. I grabbed him by the front of his shirt and picked him right off his feet. I wasn't much for fighting, not after my troubles with lima-bean-brain in first grade, and I did not want this to turn into a brawl. For a second everybody froze. I set him down and walked out of Keith Briggs's basement and went home. Not fast, not slow. I figured if the guy had wanted to, he and some of his buddies could have come after me. But nobody did.

Later I said to Stephanie, "I wish you wouldn't go to those parties."

"Why not?" She wasn't there when it happened, and I could tell by the way her jaw shot out that she wasn't just going to say okeydokey.

"Because the girls are twits and the guys are animals."

"*You* go. Are you an animal?"

"I'm higher on the evolutionary scale," I said. "And some of them are my friends."

"So how come you're friends with less evolved creatures?"

"They let me play their piano."

"I've always been crazy about animals. Especially the green-eyed kind that play the pie-anna."

Sunday afternoon.

I could have been in Chicago tonight. It would have

been easy. But I decided not to. The interstate is driving me crazy. This is not the most scenic part of the U.S.A. And then when I was studying my map, I found the Indiana Dunes National Lakeshore on Lake Michigan, and I thought, Why not? The rain had stopped and the sun was shining. No sense at all in just screaming across the country at top speed. See America First. Smell the flowers. Who knows when I'll be passing this way again.

I looked for a campground. I hated finding another one of those Yogi Bear Camp Jellystone things, with a hundred RVs parked side by side like gigantic breadboxes. But there was a state park right next to the national park, more tents than breadboxes, and cheap, too.

I set up my tent to let it dry out and started to walk. First I went to the visitors' center and learned what this place is all about. Sand was dropped here by the northwest winds, and the dunes keep moving, a little bit at a time. If I come back here again, it won't be exactly the same. But then it wouldn't be anyway, would it? I wouldn't be exactly the same either. When I see Stephanie again, I won't be the same and neither will she.

I wandered around the dunes, staring out at the lake. The lake was navy blue and the sky was pale blue, and then heavy dark clouds started rolling in and covered up the light blue and turned the navy blue to black. Watching the storm move in was like watching a print develop in the darkroom. When it seemed it could not get any darker, the first drops began to fall. They were thick and heavy as raw eggs, splattering on the ground. I ran for my tent and crawled inside, and now I'm curled up in here to wait out the storm. It has gone on for a couple of hours, and I'm cold and hungry. The tent still leaks even though I put some patching compound on the seams.

It's a beautiful place. The trouble with beautiful places is that you have to have somebody to share them with. If a tree falls in the forest and there's nobody there to hear it, does it really make the sound of a crash as it crashes? I'm that way about beautiful things—it's as if the beauty doesn't exist if there's nobody to share it with, and it's twice as beautiful if somebody's there to see it, too.

Naturally the somebody I am referring to is Stephanie. I think about her all the time. It's like a form of highway hypnosis.

Stephanie has the whitest skin I've ever seen, almost transparent. You can see a fine network of veins running through it. Her hair is long and silky and very dark, black as charcoal, and completely straight. She let it grow long so that it hangs down her back, and she has bangs cut straight across her forehead, almost to her eyebrows. And dark, dark brown eyes. She twists up her hair when she dances. She worries about her weight all the time. Dancers do that. She doesn't have one extra ounce of fat on her, all of it honed down to taut muscle over fine bones, like the wire armature a sculptor uses for making clay figures. It makes her seem light and fragile, as though she might break. But she's not fragile. She is like an Italian racing bicycle.

Other girls get pimples, other girls put on weight, but

not Steffy. She works hard to keep it that way. Absolutely nothing passes her lips that might upset her chemistry or add so much as an ounce to that delicate machinery. This has been a source of contention in our house.

She is the complete opposite of my mother in practically every way. I love Mother and we get along great. The only thing we ever really disagreed about in a major way is Dr. Grant West. You would think, then, that I would fall in love with a girl who is like my mother. But I did not.

Let me just say right up front that my mother is fat. I'm searching for a nicer word. She likes to say she is voluptuous, but she's not. Fat is the word. I don't think she was ever skinny, certainly not like Stephanie. "I'm just a Nebraska farm girl," she says, by way of excuse. "What do you expect?" And it is true that she does not have Stephanie's build. Stephanie is not tall, maybe five feet five. I tower over her by eight and a half inches. My mother is taller than Stephanie, and she has broad shoulders. "Big-boned," she says. "I can carry a lot of weight."

Just because you are tall and big-boned does not mean you have to be fat, but Mother is. She put on a lot of weight before Corky was born, and kept right on gaining.

This is one thing she and Grant argue about a lot. He says as a medical doctor and a cardiologist, it is his duty to warn her of the physical dangers of excess weight. She tells him she is his wife, not his patient. He says it looks bad for a doctor's wife, a *heart specialist's* wife, to be obese. She tells him she is not obese, that she is big-boned and can carry a lot of weight. He says it's a lack of self-discipline.

She says she is under too much stress already and has no intention of adding another stress like dieting. He wants to know what stress she's under that he isn't under even more of. She shoots back that she's got the full responsibility for three demanding children *and* a demanding husband *and* a demanding job, and that he doesn't do a damned thing to relieve that tension.

Well, I've done something about it. Now she only has *two* demanding children and one demanding husband, who is, in my unimportant and humble opinion, a jerk of the first order. I used to hope they'd split. I'd lie in bed at night and think: *Split split split*. That was before I fell in love with Stephanie. Then I started to worry that they *would* split, and Stephanie would leave again. There was always the fear that she would go back to her mother in Philadelphia.

The City of Brotherly Love. Philadelphia—our code word for making out.

But to get back to fat. Mother's fat really bothers Stephanie, too, and she sides with her father on the issue. It's one of the few serious arguments Steffy and I ever had. I complained to her because Grant had been at Mother again. She had made a sour cherry pie, in honor of George Washington's birthday. Stephanie wouldn't touch it. Grant took a sliver about the width of his fingernail and left half of that on his plate. Corky and I both went at it, and so did Mother. Then she went back for a second piece.

"You don't want that second piece of pie, Lucy," Dr. Grant said.

Mother stopped with the fork halfway to her mouth. "Yes, I do. It's good pie. Just because you happen to be neurotic on the issue of fat doesn't mean you have to make me neurotic, too. I happen to enjoy sour cherry pie. And this happens to be one of the best pies I have ever baked."

"I'm not saying it isn't a good pie, sweetie," he said, with more sugar in his voice than was in *ten* pies. "I'm saying that you simply don't need a second piece."

"You didn't say *need*. You said *want*. You said I didn't want a second piece, and I do. I truly do. I enjoy it. Look at me enjoying it!" And she made a dramatic thing out of the next forkful, rolling her eyes and smacking her lips. "I would also suggest that you have no idea at all what I want or do not want, cherry pies being an unimportant example."

"If you want to destroy your body, you're free to do it, of course," he said, getting up from the table. "But I don't have to sit and watch you do it."

Mother stared at him. "You," she said with a voice like icicles, "*smoke*."

"A pipe," he said. "Occasionally. And I do not inhale."

She went back for a third piece, not a small one.

Later Stephanie stood up for her father. "That was disgusting!" she said. "Your mother was probably very good-looking at one time, but she's a real mess right now."

"She is not a mess!" I said loudly. "She's a little overweight, I'm not denying that, but she's still pretty. A real pretty lady."

"A *little* overweight? Denny, she's gross!"

"That's easy for you to say. You're probably borderline

anorexic, but you won't admit it. Do you ever throw up after you eat? That's just as gross. Worse, even."

"Denny, it's a matter of discipline. I don't gain weight because I'm *careful*, not because I throw up. Your mother is a very nice person, but she has absolutely no self-discipline."

We went from there into her idea that I have no self-discipline either. She's probably right about that. But then I made a couple of nasty cracks about her old man, using words I will not put on this tape, and it was two days before we couldn't stand being mad at each other anymore and made up.

Sunday night. The rain let up a little while ago, and I ran over to the camp store and called home from the pay phone. I didn't want to talk to Mother and get a lot of hassling. I wasn't worried about Grant answering the phone; doctors never do, and we have our number listed under Brown so that he won't be disturbed in the middle of taking a shower or something. His beeper is always going off anyway.

Corky usually outraces everybody. She is actually pretty good at it, screening the calls carefully. "Who may I say is calling?" she asks, as though she's the maid in an English mansion. Sometimes, though it's hard to get it away from her.

It was too much to hope for that Stephanie would answer the phone. I called and Corky answered. "The West residence," she said.

"Hi, Corky. Is Stephanie there?"

"Who may I say is calling?"

"Corky, listen, it's Denny. But keep quiet for a minute, okay? Just quietly go get Stephanie, and then I'll talk to you later."

"Denny, everyone here is really mad at you," she said severely. "Where are you anyway?"

"Indiana," I said. "Now will you please get Stephanie?"

"Stephanie West is not permitted to receive any telephone calls or any other forms of communication from anyone and especially you for the rest of her life, Daddy says. My guess is two weeks for everybody else. Why is he so mad at you, Denny?"

"Your daddy isn't there now, is he? Maybe you could make an exception just this one time. It's a matter of life and death."

"Really?" Corky said, getting interested. "What're you doing, Denny?"

Getting irritated is what I was doing. I had fed a few quarters into the phone, forgetting I could have called collect, and I was going to be out of change before I talked to anybody but Corky, who was prepared to settle down for a nice long chat. "I'm in jail," I said, and immediately regretted it. Then I heard Mother's voice and Corky reporting, "Mama, it's Denny and he's in *jail*!"

"Oh my God!" Mother grabbed the phone. "Dennis, is this you? What's going on?"

"It's okay," I said. "I'm not in jail. I just told Corky that. I don't know why I said it."

"But where *are* you?"

"Somewhere in Indiana," I said. "I'm fine. I just decided to take a long camping trip."

"In Indiana? Denny, I don't understand why you'd want to go camping in Indiana. There's nothing out there."

My mother is one of those people who believes there's nothing west of Pennsylvania, now that she's left Nebraska.

I could hear Corky yelling in the background: "Mama, tell him to send me postcards! Postcards from all over!"

"When are you coming back, Denny?" Mother asked in a worried voice.

"You may remember I was kicked out," I said. "Dr. West doesn't want me back there."

"Well, Denny, he was upset, of course, but he's much calmer now. Believe me. He was upset about Stephanie. He says things he doesn't mean when he's upset."

"He said I'm a black bastard. I think he meant that."

I could hear Mother start to cry, and I was feeling like crying myself. "It was because of Stephanie. . . ."

"I didn't do anything to Stephanie. Nothing she wasn't doing, too."

"But, Denny, in our own house! He thinks you were taking advantage of the situation. Of her being here. And you know Stephanie is not a strong person."

"Stephanie is as strong as an ox. She's a dancer! She just pretends to be fragile to get around her father."

"If you hadn't taken off we could have talked about this. . . ."

"There's nothing to talk about. Mother, listen, I gotta

hang up. There's somebody waiting to use the phone. I'll call you in a few days, okay? Just don't worry about me."

As soon as I hung up it rang again. I picked it up, hoping that by some magic it was Stephanie. But it was the operator. "Deposit an additional dollar-fifty, please."

It had begun to pour again, and I got drenched on my way back to my soggy tent.

Tape 3

Monday, June 30th. Chicago.

When I woke up this morning the rain had stopped. I made peanut butter sandwiches for breakfast and took one last walk along the lakeshore. Then I pointed Mary west again, toward Eugenia Brown's.

Was it better to call first, or just show up? I thought of knocking on her front door, and when the door opened I would say, "Hello, I'm your grandson, Dennis." But how was I going to find the place? And what if she didn't like surprises like that?

So I called from a gas station, and some man answered and said Mrs. Brown was busy and wanted to know who was calling. I told him I was a friend from out of town who wanted to come by and say hello. He said, "There's a funeral going on here. Where are you now?" I told him. "Okay," he said, "write this down," and gave me directions, which exit to get off, how many blocks, how many traffic lights, certain landmarks.

It is an ordinary neighborhood, not rich and ritzy, but

the kind of place that might have been rich and ritzy a long time ago but isn't anymore. The houses look as though they had all been built about the same time. There are no lawns, but everybody has a couple of bushes in the front yard and a few flowers. Big old trees have pushed up the sidewalks and made them crack.

I found the house right away. There was a long black funeral car parked in front and a lot of ordinary cars. People in coats and ties and hats were gathered on the porch and going in and out. I wondered who had died. If it was a relative, maybe my father would be here!

I found a place to park in the next block and walked back slowly. I knew I wasn't dressed right. I had on the jeans I'd been wearing for three days, and I had been camping out and hadn't even had a good wash. I was thinking maybe I ought to go find a motel and get cleaned up, but then a tall black man with a thin mustache saw me and looked at me hard. I was staring hard back at him, because he looked sort of like the way I pictured my dad.

"You looking for somebody?" he asked.

"Mrs. Eugenia Brown."

"She's inside." He turned around and went back into the house. I climbed the steps onto the wooden porch, and a tall black woman with hair as white as cotton came to the screen door. She was dressed in a purple suit with an old-fashioned pin on the lapel. She looked at me as though maybe she recognized me, but she wasn't quite sure.

"I'm Dennis Brown, James's son," I said.

Her face crinkled into a huge smile, and she rushed

across the porch and took my face between her two hands and kissed me. Now I was really concerned, because I hadn't done much about brushing my teeth in the last couple of days either.

"Come in, come in, come in!" she said. "Everybody! Everybody, look who's here! It's James's boy, Dennis!"

People came out of the kitchen carrying cups of coffee and looked me over and smiled. They began introducing themselves and explaining how they were related, but it was all a blur to me. Then Eugenia took hold of my elbow and led me into the kitchen. I managed to whisper, "Grandmother, who died?"

"Martha, Uly's brother Leopold's wife," she said. "Let's see, that would make her your great-aunt, I believe." She lowered her voice, but maybe not enough. "You wouldn't have liked her. She was a stingy old soul, and not just with her money. Martha thought she was better than anybody else, and she was a terrible gossip in the bargain. I didn't like her much myself. But still, she's family, and somebody has to get the old girl in the ground. Leopold's been dead almost as long as Uly, and those daughters of hers can scarcely tie their own shoes, so it might as well be me who does it."

Then I got up my nerve and asked her the big question: "Is my father coming to the funeral?"

"Not that I know of. I didn't even bother to let him know she died. They were never close, and we aren't in touch often, your father and I. Haven't been for some time.

Are you?" She cocked her head like a robin and looked at me with glittery eyes.

I shook my head.

"Huh," she said. It sounded like a disgusted kind of *huh*. Then she turned businesslike. "All right, young man," she said briskly, "we've got a funeral to get done here, but a great big lad like you probably needs something to eat first. Then you get a quick shower and we're on our way to the church. Afterward everybody will be back here again for eating. Probably drinking, too, if I know this bunch. Once we're rid of them, you and I will sit down quietly, and you'll tell me all about what you're doing and where you came from and where you're going. Agreed?"

I could not imagine disagreeing with Eugenia. My mother never talked much about her, but I did remember hearing something about "Eugenia's iron hand."

"Bathroom's upstairs," she said. "Hands and face are enough for now. You can do the rest after you eat."

When I came down there was a thin ham sandwich and a glass of milk on the kitchen counter. Eugenia was outside, deciding who should ride in each car. I couldn't tell which ones were the dead woman's daughters. Nobody seemed upset or sad or crying. But maybe Eugenia wouldn't let them.

I was just washing down the last of the sandwich when the tall man with the thin mustache came in and said, "I'm to wait for you while you get cleaned up. The rest of them are going over to the funeral parlor."

I got my duffel bag out of the back of the car and hoped something in it would be clean and not too wrinkled. At least I had a toothbrush. The bathroom is the old-fashioned kind with a tub with feet. No shower and no time to run a bath, so I just splashed some water on my pits, wet down my hair, scrubbed my teeth. Checked my beard in the mirror; I had started shaving every now and then, but it wasn't time. Yanked on a long-sleeved striped shirt with a button missing and a pair of jeans with splotches of varnish from days at Gochnaur's. That reminded me of Gochy and made me homesick for just a second.

While I dressed I tried to remember the name of the guy waiting on the porch to drive me to the funeral of someone whose name I also could not remember. I followed him down the steps and into the hot sunshine. We climbed into a car parked in front of the house, a white Lincoln that smelled new, and pulled smoothly away from the curb and down the block. He had on a blue pinstripe suit and a white shirt and blue tie with a little red design. His shoes were shined.

After a while I said, "I'm sorry, but I can't remember your name."

"Greg," he said. "I'm the second son."

"My father's brother?"

"If you're James's son, yes."

"I'm James's son, all right," I said, and suddenly my heart felt lighter. This was my uncle. My family. I had more than just Mother and Corky and Stephanie.

"Could you tell me the name of the lady who died?"

"Martha Brown. You ever meet any of this family before?" I shook my head. "Not even Eugenia and Ulysses?" No. "I got time to fill you in," he said.

It took us about fifteen minutes to get to the funeral parlor, and in that time my Uncle Greg rattled off the names of the other brothers, starting with Ulysses, Jr., a lawyer who works for the city of Chicago, lives on the lakeshore, belongs to a country club. Greg is next; he owns a car dealership. Frederick, known as Fritz, is an accountant with a large corporation, one of the first blacks to reach upper-level management there. Lawrence is a journalist in Madison, Wisconsin. Then he named their wives and children. I was right; there's a whole bunch of cousins, including some who are not blood relatives but are the children of wives who were married to somebody else before.

Then there are my grandmother Eugenia's brothers and sisters, and my grandfather Ulysses's brothers and sisters. Most of them are dead, including Ulysses, but there are plenty of children. The only important member of the oldest generation directly related to me is Eugenia.

"The matriarch," Greg said. "And she doesn't let you forget it. Not for one second. Man, that old lady is in charge of what happens here. She always has been. Poor Uly, she was in charge of him, too, there at the end."

I thought that was an odd way for him to talk about his own mother. "Are you married?" I asked.

"Prettiest chick you ever did see," he said. He flashed me a gleaming smile. "I'll introduce you."

We pulled up in front of a big pink building, and Greg parked his white Lincoln next in line behind a string of expensive cars. At the front of the line was a hearse and a couple of other long black vehicles and a black limo. I had never been in a place like that before. I was curious about how they fixed up the bodies and got them ready for the funeral, and I wondered where they did that. We went down a hall and into a large room. Down in front, under a couple of spotlights, was a bronze casket with the lid open. It was lined with pale blue satin, and I could just make out that there was a body in it. There were huge bouquets of flowers everywhere, and organ music played softly in the background. Facing the coffin were rows and rows of chairs, rapidly filling up. Most of the women wore hats and gloves, and the men were all in suits.

This was a strange experience for me in another way. Every single person in that room was black. I was about to add, "Except me." I had never in my memory been in a place where everybody was black. Maybe when I was a little kid, I might have been somewhere with my dad. He and Mother had black friends when they lived in New York, Mother said; she still gets Christmas cards from some of them. But I was too young to remember any of that. Once in a while I met some blacks—there were a few at the college in our town—but being with a whole roomful was a totally new thing for me.

"We'll go pay our respects," Greg said, and I followed him to the front of the room and got in line to file past the coffin. I looked inside. There was a little shriveled up black lady in there, mostly covered up with a puffy satin blanket. A pair of hands, tiny as a child's, were folded on top of the satin. "Well, that's Aunt Martha," Greg said under his breath.

I stared for as long as I could before the line moved on. It was the first time I had ever seen a dead body. I wondered what she looked like when she was alive.

Three women wearing black dresses almost exactly alike stood next to the coffin, shaking hands with everybody and turning now and then to gaze in the coffin at the dead woman. Eugenia hovered around behind them. I took them to be Martha's three daughters.

"Let's go sit down," Greg said, leading the way to a pair of seats in the third row next to a woman in a flowered dress. Her skin was almost as light as mine, and she was what you would call spectacular. "My wife, Bunny," he said, and Bunny turned on a five-hundred-watt smile and patted the seat next to her. "This is James's son Dennis," Greg said. She squeezed my hand. When we were sitting down, he whispered to me, "Didn't I tell you?"

"You're right," I said. "She's the prettiest chick I've ever seen."

Now that was an outright lie. When it comes to chicks, I'll take Stephanie any time. Also, when you are seventeen it is very hard to appreciate beauty in somebody so much older. Still, she was something. Very big—buxom, I think is the word. And that flowered dress, red and blue and yellow flowers blooming wildly all over, and shiny red shoes and a matching purse. With everybody else dressed in somber colors, she really stood out. I could tell that Greg loved having a wife who attracted so much attention.

The organ that had been playing softly in the background now swelled up dramatically, and a grizzle-haired man swept in in a black robe with velvet bands on the flowing sleeves, put on his half-glasses, peered at us, and said, "Let us pray." There was a little rustling and then quiet while everybody settled into praying.

This is something I don't know anything about. Mother had some idea of packing me off to Sunday School when we first moved to the Burg, but she changed her mind and said it was up to me. Naturally I said no. She hadn't been to church in years, she said. It was nothing but a bunch of hypocrites, and the worst of it had been right after she and my father were married.

They went to church together a few times, because she had been brought up to go to church and it was a habit with her, but nobody talked to them. They figured the preacher had to notice them, because he was standing at the door shaking hands with everybody after the service and wishing them a good day. My mother and dad shuffled along in the line, hanging on to each other's hands.

"You could feel people leaving a space around us," Mother said. As they got up closer to the preacher, they heard him making a big fuss over visitors and newcomers, telling them to come back. He mentioned a special supper they were having later that week and urged the other visitors to join the "church family" for that. Then it was Mother and Dad's turn. The preacher, a white man, shook my mother's hand and started to make a nice welcome speech to her, but Mother said, "And this is my husband, James Brown." The preacher's face turned to ice water, Mother told me. "He shook your dad's hand, mumbled 'good morning,' and looked away. That was it. No signing the visitors' book, no invitation to the supper. We didn't go back."

"But there are lots of churches," I said. "Are they all like that?"

"Maybe not all, but baby, how many times do you want to get your face slapped? We tried a couple of others before that one. None was quite that bad, but none made us welcome either. It wasn't that your dad was black, it was that he's black and I'm white. People just can't stand that."

"How come? What's wrong with it?"

"Nothing. Not one thing. But there are people in this world, and a lot of them go to church every Sunday, who believe that blacks are inferior to whites. Knowing that a black man is having sex with a white woman makes them furious. They come completely unglued. More than when it's the other way around—black woman, white man. I don't think they even know exactly why. Maybe they don't admit it to themselves. But I'll tell you, Denny, once you've seen that look of revulsion on somebody's face, you never forget it."

I know there is supposed to be a God, and that he had a son who was born at Christmas and killed on a cross on Good Friday and came back to life on Easter. And there is something called the Holy Spirit, but I have no idea what that is about. I know some people think God made the world in six days. The Ten Commandments are okay, although I don't understand them very well.

And I sure do not know anything about praying. The thing is, I don't know if it works, and what's the use of doing something if it doesn't work? For instance, if you've got two armies fighting against each other, or even two football teams, and they both pray to be the winner, only one is going to get their prayers answered. So what good did it do the losers to pray? I don't understand that. And that is just the beginning of what I don't understand about God and religion.

"Let us pray," the preacher said, but I didn't have to worry about the "us." He had a long prayer of his own, and we listened to him telling God to take good care of the faithful departed. There was more praying and some singing, and a long speech by the preacher about all the good Martha Brown had done during her long life. It didn't sound like the same person Eugenia told me about.

Finally it ended, and we all piled into cars again and drove in a slow, somber procession led by a motorcycle cop to a cemetery. When the final prayers had been said, the last of Aunt Martha was lowered into the ground and her daughters in the black dresses tossed a few flowers onto her coffin.

While the cars were filling up again I wandered around and read the names and dates and inscriptions on some of the gravestones. Eugenia walked over to a tall white marble monument and laid some flowers on the grass beside it.

That would be Grandfather Ulysses's grave. She looked small and lonely, standing there with her head bowed, and I thought about going over to stand with her, but I didn't. I don't know her very well, and it would have felt funny. I am not the kind of person who goes around hugging and kissing people I don't know, even when they're relatives, and I don't like it when people I don't know hug and kiss me.

This is something you grow up with. Some families do a lot of touching. Ours doesn't. Mother said she didn't get much hugging when she was growing up, and so she doesn't do much. Neither does Grant. So how come, then, Stephanie and I, children of people who hardly touch, like to touch each other so much? We were always maneuvering to be near each other. We almost couldn't keep our hands off each other, which was a real problem. I'm not talking about heavy-duty stuff, I'm talking about being able to feel Steffy's cool, smooth skin and to put my hand on her silky hair. She likes to touch my back, gently stroking the valley where the muscles connect to the spine. We have this thing we call "skinlove," just stroking each other's skin—arms, wrists, backs. I could not get enough of that, and thinking about it makes me ache.

As soon as we were out of the cemetery, the whole mood changed. Back at the house, the dining room table was loaded with food—turkey, ham, roast beef, and a row of casseroles and bowls of salad and baskets of rolls, with little saucers of mustard and mayonnaise. You loaded up your plate and went outside. Long tables had been set up in the backyard and covered with sheets of white paper. There were little bunches of flowers on each table.

I followed Greg and Bunny, not knowing what else to do. Greg brought me a bottle of beer and a glass.

I will not say that it was the first beer I have ever had in my life. It was not. When I got together with Keith Briggs and the guys, there was always beer, and I am not so virtuous that I refused to drink any. Sure I drank. Everybody did. Sometimes I even got wasted and felt like a pile of garbage all the next day, my head thick and thumping, my guts soggy and squeezing. But Stephanie pretty much ended that. "Why on earth would you want to put poison into your body?" she asked.

"It's not cyanide," I said. "It's beer."

"It's a matter of quantity, not kind," she said. "Alcohol is as much of a poison as cyanide. It just takes more of it to do you in. And I have seen you getting done in enough to point out that it is not improving the quality of your life."

"But it's fun," I argued. "It's a lot of fun to get wasted once in a while."

"Have you ever seen yourself when you're wasted? *Listened* to yourself? I should make a video of you. You think you're suave and clever, and you're just gross and dumb."

Of course, just to show her, I went out and got wasted at the next opportunity, but the whole time I thought I was being suave and clever, I kept hearing her voice saying I was gross and dumb. Furthermore she wouldn't speak to me for three days afterward, and I decided it wasn't worth it. Not at all. So no more beer.

But now here I am in Chicago, and with a houseful of strangers who are my relatives, Stephanie is hundreds of miles away, and my uncle has just handed me a bottle of beer. I took it and held it. Its coolness felt good in my hand.

"Now we're going to meet some people."

Greg led me around from group to group. "This is Dennis, James's son," he said, and he'd tell me their names and how they were related, but of course I couldn't remember any of it. What I was really looking for were my cousins, people my own age. I got stared at plenty, people asking me how James was doing. I guess they didn't realize that I probably know less than they do. Then I felt somebody's arm around my waist. It was Bunny.

"Somebody here wants to meet you," she said, and marched me away from the table, her arm around me like a clamp. "My daughter, Roxanne. Come this way."

We went back inside to the kitchen where a beautiful woman was slicing a chocolate cake into perfect wedges. She looked like a model or something, she was that pretty. She was wearing a pink dress with two little thin straps over her dark brown shoulders and a full skirt and a wide belt striped in all kinds of colors. When she saw us she licked icing off her finger and smiled a lazy smile. Her long fingernails were painted dark pink. How come I hadn't seen her before, at the funeral, where everybody except her mother was wearing something somber?

"Roxy, this is Dennis Brown. He just arrived this morning from Pittsburgh."

"Vicksburg," I said. "Pennsylvania." I couldn't seem to stop staring at her.

Roxanne shook my hand and smiled again. A wide mouth, with lots of white teeth. "Welcome to Chicago. Excuse the chocolate."

"Thanks."

"I'll be right back," Bunny said. "I want to go see what that husband of mine is up to." She left us alone in the kitchen.

"Sit down, Dennis," Roxanne said. I pulled out a kitchen chair, still staring at her. Then I saw her watching me, and I switched the stare to my own hands, which were twitching in my lap. She appeared amused.

"Did you come all this way for Martha's funeral?"

I shook my head and finally got my tongue to work. "No. I'm on my way to California to see my father. I stopped in to say hello to my grandmother. I didn't know Aunt Martha. I don't know any of these people."

"You didn't miss much as far as Martha was concerned. One of those miserable people who only got happy when she was making everybody else miserable. Shall I tell you about some of the rest of them? They're an odd bunch, actually."

"That's a weird way to talk about your family."

"Well, it's not really my family. My mother married Greg a year ago, although she's been with him for fifteen years, waiting for him to divorce his first wife. I don't have much to do with any of them. I came over today to help with the food and set up the tables while the rest of you were paying your last respects."

"I knew I hadn't seen you at the funeral." I took a swig of beer from the bottle. It had gotten warm and it tasted terrible, but I didn't know what else to do with myself. "You cooked all this food? It looks wonderful." Somewhere outside was my plate, but I hadn't even gotten to taste it. And I was starving.

"Thank you. I'm studying to be a chef. Or at least that's the general idea. Right now I'm working part-time for a little cafe while I'm in school. Someday I'm going to have my own restaurant. That's my dream. And I do things like this. Weddings, funerals, bar mitzvahs—you name it. If you want food, Roxanne will be there. What are your life plans, Dennis?"

That question again. "I don't know," I said. "I'm trying to figure that one out. You're lucky, knowing what you want to do with your life."

"I always know what I want." I had been swigging the warm beer again, but there was something about her voice that made me take a fast swallow and shoot a glance at her. She was looking right at me, with a kind of a deliberate smile.

"How old are you?" she asked.

"Eighteen," I lied, but not by very much. "How old are you?"

"Twenty-four," she said. "How much do you know about Chicago?" She was leaning forward, her elbows propped on the kitchen counter, and I could smell her faint perfume.

"Nothing. I just got here."

"But you've been here before, haven't you?"

"No."

"Are you free tomorrow? I'll take you on a tour."

"I'm free tomorrow," I said.

"Good. I'll pick you up at ten." She stood up. She was very tall, like her mother. "Now I have to go see about dessert for all these folks."

She had made lemon pudding in addition to chocolate mocha cake. I had both. I found some of my cousins and sat with them. There was only one my age, and she was a jock. She wanted to know what sports I played, and when I told her I didn't do much, she ignored me. There were some little girls running around, one a poor homely thing with huge buck teeth who tried to get me to play Parcheesi. If there's one thing I hate, it's games. I had seen a great big grand piano in the living room, and I kept hoping somebody would sit down and play it. Nobody did. I was itching to go fool around with it, but I wasn't going to be the one to start.

People began to leave. I didn't know what I was supposed to do. Eugenia said we were going to talk. I didn't know if she wanted me to stay there, or if she thought I was going to keep on driving. Nobody else had invited me to come. Greg asked, "How long are you going to be in town?" and I said, "Depends."

What it depended on was what was wrong with my car, which was now going *klunk . . . klunk* even louder. It seemed to have something to do with the steering, or maybe the brakes. I was going to have to pull the wheels and see what was going on there.

Then the house was empty. The women had gotten involved in cleaning the place up, collecting the plates and so on, and the men had folded up the tables and chairs and taken them back to the rental place. There had been more than forty people, and then it was just Eugenia and me.

"I'm going to rest for an hour, Dennis," she said. "And then you and I will have a cup of tea and get acquainted."

Now the hour is almost up. I'll bet she's right on time, but that's the only thing I'm betting on.

Tape 4

Still Monday, the 30th. Late.

Grandmother Eugenia was back from her nap exactly one hour later, full of life. She boiled water in a teakettle and poured it into a china pot. She set the pot and two cups and saucers on a tray with a sugar bowl and cream pitcher and a plate of thin slices of lemon with a clove stuck in each one. I followed her into a room with dark woodwork and heavy drapes and the Steinway grand.

Eugenia said, "Give it a few minutes to steep. Meanwhile, tell me about yourself."

I took a deep breath. "Well," I said, "I'm on my way to California to find my father."

She nodded. "When was the last time you saw him?"

"A few years ago. Five or six, I guess."

"James is the Eternal Boy, *puer eternis*. A psychological type, not given to taking responsibility well. But a charmer, a charmer." She said it as though she were talking to herself. "Does he write to you, at least?"

"Once in a while," I said. Another lie. He hasn't written to me in a long time, but I guess that's because I don't write to him.

"And your mother? How is she?"

"She's fine."

"Is she still married to the doctor?"

"Yes. They have a little girl named Corky. Did you know about that?"

"I think James mentioned it. How old is the child?"

"Six. She's real smart. Probably a genius."

"Does the doctor have any children?"

I was getting uncomfortable. I wanted to get off this subject, quick. "He has one daughter, Stephanie. But listen, Grandmother, I don't want to talk about the West family. I want to hear about the Browns. I don't know anything at all about this side of the family."

That pleased her. She poured tea into cups so thin you could see light through them. "Lemon or cream?"

"Both," I said. "Please."

"Both?" She hesitated, and her hand wavered over the cup. That's when I noticed that her hands are all gnarled and knotted, the knuckles big, bony knobs.

"Lemon *and* cream," I said, and soon as it was out of my mouth I knew I had made a mistake, but what do I know about drinking tea?

"Perhaps you'd like to help yourself then."

I speared a circle of lemon with a tiny silver fork and managed to drop it in my tea without splashing. Next three cubes from the fat sugar bowl, picked out with miniature tongs. Then I poured in the cream. Instant curdle. I pretended nothing had happened, and I think Eugenia was pretending not to smile.

The room has a dark carpet with a pattern of flowers around the border, and the sofa and three chairs are all upholstered in something that itched my skin where my bare arms touched it. The woodwork is dark brown, and the walls are papered in little sprigs of green on a tan background. Lace curtains hang behind dark-green velvet drapes. It is the kind of room that soaks up all the sound. Even our voices sounded soft, wrapped in velvet. The one magnificent thing in the room is the Steinway.

Eugenia fixed her own cup of tea and settled back in a deep armchair. "So you want to know about the Brown family," she said. "And how about the Carters? Are you interested in the Carters as well?"

"I'm sorry, I don't know who you mean."

"The Carters are my side of the family. That's the Anderson connection."

"Excuse me?"

"Marian Anderson is my side of the family. Paul Robeson was on the Brown side."

I knew I was supposed to recognize those names. I remember Mother saying something like "Anderson on one side, Robeson on the other. James was bracketed by fame." But I didn't know what she meant by that. Grandmother could tell immediately that I didn't know who she was talking about.

"Oh, Lordy, Lordy. You've really been brought up white, haven't you? Nothing wrong with that, except that it leaves out half your heritage. Probably the more interesting half, and certainly the more artistic half, if you'll forgive my saying so."

I sat still, not saying a word. I hadn't thought about that, being brought up white. Naturally—it was my white mother who brought me up, not my black father, who didn't bother to stay around.

"Dennis, I don't think it's any secret that I was very much opposed to your parents' marriage. Of course they didn't ask my opinion, they simply went ahead and did it, in the way young people have, and then told us about it afterward. Your grandfather Ulysses—I'm sorry you never got to know him, you would have found him fascinating— anyway, he had a heart attack soon after your parents came to tell us they were married. It's not that I don't like your mother. She's an attractive, intelligent young woman. She was a young woman then, of course, not so young anymore. It was clear that she was in love with James, and James was in love with her. But marriages like that rarely work out."

"Why? Why wouldn't it work, if they loved each other?"

"Because there were too many differences between them, too many gaps to bridge. Marriage is always hard work in the best of circumstances, and this was not an ideal way to start. I told them then it wouldn't last."

She didn't mention the fact that my mother was pregnant when they married, and neither did I. That's something I don't like to think about—that I wasn't planned and maybe wasn't even wanted. "I still don't see why it's so hard for people of different races to get married."

"That was not my primary objection, although they must have known they'd be in trouble from the first with that. But sometimes adversity draws people together. You know, the nastiness, the comments, the *looks* I'm sure they got just walking down the street together."

Mother used to tell me stories about that.

"If the racial thing wasn't your primary objection, then what was?"

"Dennis, you're a nice boy, but there are certain things you just aren't aware of. Class difference is what I'm talking about. I don't mean to sound cruel, but you're obviously searching for something, and you're certainly old enough to know the truth. The fact is that your mother, lovely person that I'm sure she is, is simply from a different social class than ours. She doesn't have the background or the breeding that the Browns or the Carters have. Your mother's family is, to put it bluntly, redneck. Everyone in our family, every single one, has a college education. The University of Chicago, Harvard, Princeton. Most are professional people or successful in business. That's quite different from a dirt farmer in Nebraska who thinks all niggers should have been kept in slavery."

Wow—what a snob! I watched her sip her tea and set the cup back on the saucer. "My mother has everything done for her Ph.D. except writing the dissertation," I said very carefully. "She'd have done that, too, except she got married and had me instead."

"A common failing of women, making that choice. I managed both. I had two children when I finished up my degree in social work. And my grandfather was born in a slave cabin in Mississippi, so you can't say we've had it handed to us. We've worked for it, pulled ourselves up by our bootstraps. Even in my generation we were a family of doctors and lawyers and teachers. Then in the next generation, your father's generation, they all became professionals, too, or own their own businesses, all except your daddy, and he decided he'd be a musician."

"What's wrong with that?"

"I don't want you to think I'm not proud of him, Dennis, because I am! He used to sit in this living room and play on that piano—Mozart, Chopin, Beethoven, Debussy—and the tears would roll down my cheeks, it was that beautiful. He could have had a fine life as a teacher, but that's not what he wanted. He wanted to be a performer, and that's a much more difficult row to hoe. There are sacrifices to be made. He went to Paris and began to play jazz. I knew that would be the end of his career. It was."

"Maybe the end of the career that *you* wanted," I said. She looked at me sharply, those bright robin's eyes. Maybe I sounded rude. I was getting mad, but I also wanted to hear what she had to say. If I'm going to figure out who I am, then I may have to listen to some things I don't want to hear. "He's still playing the piano, isn't he?"

"In cocktail lounges, Dennis! In *bars*! A man who could bring tears to your eyes playing the *Pathétique* at the age of twelve!" Tears were glittering in her eyes.

I tried to change the subject. "Tell me about Anderson and Robeson, Grandmother," I said.

"Incredible ignorance," she muttered, mostly to herself, refilling her teacup and mine. I stuck to sugar, no lemon, no cream, no curdles. "Inexcusable, really. Next you'll be telling me you've never heard of Martin Luther King."

"I'm not *that* bad."

"How long are you planning to stay?" she asked abruptly.

"Not very long. I have to do some work on my car, and then I'll get back on the road again." I wondered if she was anxious to get rid of me. I sure wasn't fulfilling her idea of what a grandson should be. And here I am, the only grandson. Every one of the other umpty-ump grandchildren is a girl, but James, baby of the family—the spoiled brat, to hear Grandmother talk about him—is the only one to produce a son. And the son is only half black.

I began to guess that Eugenia, crotchety old snob that she is, loves James more than any of the rest, even though he writes to her only on her birthday, calls her only at Christmas, and hasn't come to see her in five years. Three of her sons live in Chicago; Lawrence, the journalist, in Madison, Wisconsin, comes home every month or so. They take care of her like a queen since their father died. But who does she seem to think about most?

You're not supposed to have favorites in a family, but everybody I know does. I could see that in the families I knew back in the Burg. Sometimes the father would have one favorite and the mother a different favorite, which is okay when there are just two kids and each kid has a champion. But it's bad when there are three, and one is left out; if there is more than one unfavorite in the family, those guys can band together.

When Corky was born I was a little jealous of her, but it didn't last long because Mother didn't make me feel that I didn't matter anymore. When I fell in love with Stephanie I was glad Corky got so much attention, and Grant and Mother didn't notice what we were doing, where we went, how much time we spent together.

If I ever get married and have a family, I won't have a favorite. I'm going to love everybody exactly the same, even if one of them behaves really badly. I can imagine that right now Mother is having a hard time loving me as much as she does Corky.

"More talent in this little finger . . ." Eugenia said, holding up her hand.

I think I know why he doesn't come to see her. I think he's ashamed. He knows he's her favorite but that he doesn't live up to what she expects of him. She wants him to be performing Mozart on a concert stage or teaching music at a college, and now all he plays is jazz. She probably doesn't think of jazz as real music. So it must be easier for him to stay away.

If I ever get married and have a family, I'm not going to try to force my kids to have a certain kind of job or live in a certain kind of way.

When Mother used to lecture me because I was bringing home such horrible report cards, and fuss about whether I was going to have good enough grades to get into college, and worry about what was going to happen to my future, I'd tell her, "The trouble is, you want me to work for an insurance company or something. You want me to be *secure*."

"Of course I want you to be secure. I want you to do what's good for you, but I also don't want you starving in a garret or sleeping in the street."

"Did George Sand starve in a garret? Everybody who does anything adventurous starves in a garret at least part of the time. I bet you on that." I had to look up "garret" in the dictionary. It's an attic.

"My reaction is perfectly normal and sensible," Mother said. "No mother wants her child to starve."

"I'm not going to starve. I just don't know what I want to do yet."

So I sat in the dark living room with Eugenia and bet I could figure out what was going through her head. Here is the only grandson, only son of the black sheep of the family, and she's wondering about me. Is there any hope for this one? she's thinking. I decided to bail out.

"So tell me about my famous relatives, Paul Robeson and Anderson, what's her name, Marian," I said. If I was

going to be a disgrace, I might as well learn something.
The switch worked.

"To begin with Paul Robeson," she said. "He and your
grandfather were second cousins. He was terribly controversial, you see, even in Uly's family. Paul was the son
of a runaway slave. Do you know *anything* about black
history, Dennis? The underground railway and so forth?
I'm going to see to it that you have some books to take
with you. You don't know anything about yourself until
you know your roots."

"I watched that program about roots on television," I
said. She didn't need to act as though I come from another
planet. I do know *something* about what's going on in the
world. And why do I have to know all about black history?
I never liked history, dates and battles and names. Boring
stuff. I didn't say that, but she looked as though she knew
exactly what I was thinking.

"Paul is a distant relative of yours, remember. He got a
law degree at Columbia, but what he really wanted was to
be an actor. He played the title role in Eugene O'Neill's
play *Emperor Jones* in 1925. They made a movie of it in the
thirties, and was *that* controversial! In one scene he killed
a white prison guard who had tried to force him to beat a
black prisoner. It would have been the first time a black
was shown killing a white on the screen in America, and
they cut the scene. It made Paul mad, and for a long time
he didn't want to make any more moving pictures. I remember him saying, 'You bet they'll never let me play a

part in a film in which a Negro is on top.' He said they only ever showed Negroes solving their problems by singing their way to glory. His exact words.

"So your grandfather and I got on the train and went to New York to see his cousin Paul. What a magnificent man! I will never forget that voice, or forget him singing 'Ol' Man River.' Jerome Kern wrote that especially for Paul and his big bass voice." She pushed herself stiffly up out of her chair. "You might as well listen to some records."

She searched through a shelf of records until she found what she was looking for. The phonograph was old-fashioned and the record was pretty scratchy, but the voice was amazing. You could feel it in the pit of your stomach.

"He played Othello, too," she said, easing back down into her chair. "I'm not going to ask you if you've read Shakespeare's play, although goodness knows you should have. If I can find a copy I'm going to put it in your bag with some other books. In case you don't know the plot, it's about a love affair between a Moor, which is a black person, and a white woman, Desdemona. Every black actor who ever lived has wanted to play Othello, and believe me, there have been some good ones. Paul first performed it in London in 1930, the first black in seventy years to play the role. They used to take a white actor and darken him up a little, pretending he was sort of an Arab. But Paul did some research and found out that Shakespeare himself saw Othello as an African, a man of noble heritage. After Shakespeare's time the slave trade had begun, and Africans were seen as slaves, never as kings.

"For years American producers were scared to death to put up the money for a Broadway production of *Othello*. They said Americans would never go to a theater to see a black man play a love scene with a white woman. But finally they did it, in 1943. It broke every record in New York for a Shakespearean production, and then they took it on the road. We saw it here, of course. The theater was packed every night. When it finally closed in 1945 they said a half million people had seen it. Except in the South, of course. Paul wouldn't play to segregated audiences. I wish you could have seen him, Dennis. He was magnificent. But then all that ended."

"Ended?" Eugenia had me completely enthralled with her story. "What happened?"

"Oh, the government decided he was a Communist. He made some speeches that got everyone upset. Even in this family we argued about whether he was a Commie or not. The government took away his passport and destroyed his career. And when his son, Paul Junior, married a white girl, well that was *it*. A couple of months later there were riots when he tried to give a concert. A sad, sad thing."

She sank into a silence that lasted so long I wondered if she had forgotten I was there. After a while she drifted back. "I'm going to excuse myself now, Dennis. I've had a long day. Tillie will come and show you where you're to sleep, and she'll make sure you have something to eat. I'll see you in the morning. I get up very early, but that needn't bother you. Breakfast is at seven."

She levered herself up out of her chair again and

marched slowly to the door. After she had gone, I turned on the old record player again and filled the room with the powerful voice of Paul Robeson, whose ancestors were also mine.

I sat for a long time in Eugenia's chair with arms shaped like loaves of bread, listening to Robeson and soaking up his voice. That's when it began to sink in that my great-great-grandparents, way back somewhere, came from Africa. That they had been slaves. Paul Robeson said Othello had been a king, a king in Africa. I wondered if any of our people had been kings and queens, Robeson's and Eugenia's and mine. Seeing something on TV is nothing, nothing at all like listening to your own grandmother tell you about your people.

Eugenia said Paul Robeson died in Philadelphia in 1976. She had visited him and his sister there. All roads lead to Philadelphia. Mention that name and my mind leaps: Stephanie. Stephanie is in another world now; I had left her world and was traveling in new spaces. I remember her telling me that her grandmother was a member of the Daughters of the American Revolution, a bunch of old ladies whose ancestors had fought in the Revolutionary War. Big deal. On one side of the family Stephanie could trace her family all the way back to the *Mayflower*.

"So what?" I said to her once, because I think she was secretly proud of it and was just telling me about it to get a rise out of me, which she did. "Everybody in this country except the Indians had their ancestors come over on a boat. Your mother's came on an English boat, my mother's came on a Swedish boat. They both probably got seasick and threw up. What's to brag about?" I realize now that I only talked about my *mother's* ancestors, not my father's, who probably came in chains in the hold of a slave ship.

"Everybody needs something to be proud of," Stephanie told me. "For some people it's their ancestry."

"That's only if they're not doing anything themselves to be proud of," I said.

"You'll really enjoy *this* then, Denny," she said. "My mom the Duchess still belongs to her college sorority. She goes to alumnae meetings, and they write letters of recommendation about young ladies they want to join their sorority. She has these songs she sings about dear old Kappa Kappa Gamma."

I know about sororities and fraternities, because the Burg is a college town and there are a bunch of fraternity houses on the campus and scattered around town. Every now and then the local police are called in to break up some wild party.

"Grant still has a picture of his Yale crew, hanging in the bedroom," I reminded her. "Do you think we'll still be living in the past when we're as old as our parents?"

She shuddered. "I hope not. I intend always to live totally in the present. In the *moment*," she said, her fingers buried in my hair.

My mother lives in the future. She's always trying to see way down the road and predict what's going to happen. She assumes it will be something bad, that something terrible is going to happen and she won't be able to control it. But she thinks if she worries enough about it, then she'll be prepared for the worst. But it doesn't work. She's never ready.

"I heard somebody say in a movie once, I think it was Robert Redford, that the world is curved so we won't be able to see too far down the road. I think that's beautiful, don't you, Denny?"

I was running my fingers along the curve of her ear. "Who? Robert Redford? He's not my type."

"Denny, be serious. I want to be serious, and I can't be if you aren't."

"Why can't you be serious and me be crazy? Who says we both have to be the same way at the same time?"

"Nobody," she said, moving away from me, but somehow I had stuck my finger in that bubble and popped it and now it was gone.

Living in the past is a mistake. But finding out about your past, the past that made you what you are, that couldn't be a mistake, could it?

I turned the record over and listened to more Paul Robeson. Then I noticed that I wasn't by myself. Tillie had come in silently in old slippers and stood in the shadows. She's a tiny, wizened woman who lives here with Eugenia. I remember my dad mentioning her, that Tillie had come to live with them when he was a little kid, to help out when Eugenia was sick with something for a long time, and never went home again. Maybe she didn't have a home to go to. Anyway, she was still there.

"Would you like a sandwich, Dennis? There's plenty left from this afternoon."

I was so hungry I felt hollow. I went with her into the kitchen. It was like stepping into a time machine, everything bright and shiny but really old, from long before they started making refrigerators and stoves anything but white. The cupboards are old-fashioned, too, and the floor has a patterned linoleum on it. The room could be in a museum, if they have museums for things from 1950.

Tillie opened the ancient refrigerator. Inside were a half-dozen plastic containers. You couldn't tell what was in any of them. "We gave most of it away," Tillie said. "Your grandmother and I don't eat much, and it just goes bad."

Moving very slowly—it was kind of painful to watch her, because she is so bent over and frail-looking—Tillie took out one bowl, closed the door, shuffled over to the counter, which is a long way off in the big old-fashioned kitchen, set the bowl down, worked at prying the lid off, and shuffled slowly back for the next thing.

"I'll help," I said. "But I'll just eat whatever's in the first couple of bowls."

I was instantly sorry I said that, because the first one was potato salad, not a favorite of mine, and the second was some kind of mixture that I couldn't identify by look or smell. There was also a purplish jello salad with fruit and nuts in it, another bad idea. Tillie fussed around in slow motion, fixing up a tray with a cloth napkin and a glass of ice water and a bunch of silverware.

"You don't need to bother, Tillie. I can do this myself. And I'll clean it up afterward too."

Tillie looked at me as though she didn't believe a word of it—either that I was capable of making my own sandwich or had any intention of cleaning up. I stuck my head back in the ancient refrigerator and searched out some of the leftover meat, wrapped in waxed paper like a gift. I lined up six slices of bread and piled a few slices of ham, beef, and turkey on each one, stacked lettuce and tomato on the other three slices, and cemented them together in pairs with mayo. Tillie watched me with her arms folded. I stacked them on the little plate she had set out for me. Then I loaded a second plate with stuff from the bowls— potato salad, the purple gunk, the unidentifiable substance —but only a little of each.

"Where do you want me to take this?" I asked her.

Tillie studied the loaded tray. "Out in the backyard," she said.

I followed her through the kitchen door and sat down at an old iron table on a hard iron chair, ready to dive into the pile of food. Tillie was still watching me.

"You're James's boy," she said.

I already had my mouth full, so I just nodded.

"I remember when your father was just a little bit of a thing," she said. "I came here before the war, you know, and I've been here ever since. James was born on Pearl Harbor Day, December 7, 1941. We always teased him about that, you know. At least nobody would ever forget his birthday, we said. We got the news that the Japanese had bombed Pearl Harbor just about the time we got the news that James was born. I hadn't been here very long then. Eugenia had been sick. She was never very strong, and she had a hard time of it. The doctors kept her in bed through most of it. And then after James was born, I stayed on to help take care of him while Eugenia got her strength back."

I wanted to hear more about my father, but for some reason I asked her, "You got a family, Tillie?"

"No," she said, dabbing at her face with a lace handkerchief. "No, I never married. This family is all the family I've had, and all I ever want. I am devoted to Eugenia, and I was devoted to Ulysses. It was my pleasure to watch their children grow up and leave home and have children of their own, and it's my pleasure to have them come back to visit. Some of them, of course, are better than *others*," she said, and I could tell by the sharp way she said it that she was referring to my father.

"James was such a solemn child," she said. "Such a serious little person! He was so much younger than the older ones—Lawrence was six when James was born—that it was almost like he was an only child. Ulysses and Eugenia just doted on that boy. Eugenia was close to forty when James came along, and Ulysses was nearly fifty. You're too old! I remember thinking when they told me about this child, but of course it wasn't my place to *say* anything. Ulysses was scared to death it was going to kill Eugenia, and to tell you the truth, it's a wonder it didn't. He waited on her hand and foot. I never saw anything like it, the way that man doted on her. It was a joy to see.

"When your father was born, he was their precious jewel. Nothing was too good for him. He was a very affectionate child, always climbing on Eugenia's lap. I think Ulysses resented him, because Eugenia paid so much attention to him. She doted on the boy the way Ulysses doted on *her*. She pushed him into music, you see, made that the focus."

"Pushed him?" I asked her. "You mean he wasn't talented?"

"I didn't say he wasn't," she said, sounding annoyed. "But she's the one who bought that great big expensive piano and got him off to lessons and made sure he practiced. She's the one who made sure he had big recitals. She was always dreaming of James in New York, playing at Carnegie Hall. She talked about it all the time. 'When James plays at Carnegie Hall . . .'"

"Did he play there?"

"No. I think he *could* have, if he'd wanted to. But it wasn't what he wanted. He wanted to play jazz." She wrinkled up her nose when she said it. "All that money spent on fancy lessons, and that beautiful piano sitting in there that cost your grandfather an arm and a leg, I can tell you that much, but Eugenia talked him into it."

I was well into my second sandwich before I remembered some manners. "Don't you want to sit down, Tillie?"

"Thank you," she said, and perched on the other hard

iron chair. "Now this is not to criticize your grandmother, but Eugenia has always thought a little too highly of herself and put a little too much emphasis on material goods, in my opinion. If she had just let James alone, he would have stayed around, not gone running off to Paris, and he could have played whatever music made him happy and then he'd be here, close to his mother instead of moving all over the world. I've told her many times, 'Eugenia,' I've said, 'you brought it all on yourself, you and your hifalutin ideas.' She sees herself as society, you know, and that's dangerous."

It was dark now in the garden, only a little glow from the yellow porch light shining on Tillie's wrinkled black face. She's lived in this house for at least forty-five years and maybe even longer, and yet she doesn't seem to like Eugenia very much. Then I asked her about my grandfather, and I understood why.

Her face softened; it had been very pinched when she talked about Eugenia. "He was a saint," she said softly. "That's all I can tell you. A saint."

Uh-oh, I thought; Tillie was in love with Ulysses. I wondered if she always had been, and how he felt about her. He had been dead now for ten years or so. It must have been easier to stay here with Eugenia than to go find another home, but there would be reminders of Ulysses everywhere, always firing up her memories. I wondered if Eugenia knew about it. I wondered if Tillie and Ulysses had ever . . . you know. Probably not.

It used to be different, Mother says; people didn't just

jump into bed whenever they felt like it, the way they do now. I don't know about that. I think people have been making love whether they're supposed to or not since the beginning of time. They just talk about it more now, and put it on television. I could imagine how hard it must have been for Tillie to be living in the same house with somebody she loved and not be able to be with him. I mean, I am an expert on that, aren't I? It made me feel more friendly toward Tillie.

"I'll show you where you're going to sleep, Dennis," she said. "Then I'm going to bed myself."

She led me upstairs and down a narrow hall to this back bedroom overlooking the yard where we had been sitting. "This was James's room," she said. "I think you'll like staying here." She looked at me for a minute before she left. "It's a good thing Eugenia's sight is failing," she said. "If she could see how much you resemble James, it would break her heart."

She left me alone.

Tape 5

Tuesday evening, July 1st.

Everything in this room belongs to James Dennis Brown. His high school and college diplomas are framed and hanging on the wall. There's a snapshot, enlarged, of Eugenia the way she must have looked about thirty years ago, standing next to a distinguished-looking man who is probably Ulysses and a tall skinny kid. No doubt about who he is. There are pictures of the skinny kid at the piano, and a school picture in coat and tie, his hair cut short above his ears. My skin is much lighter, but the features are pretty much alike. And the green eyes.

I was tired last night, but I went through the room, examining everything. Some clothes are still hanging in the closet, clothes he must have worn when he was about my age. I peeled down to my shorts and tried some of them on. They are the kind of things Stephanie loves. She's into funky old clothes, and these are definitely funky, probably from the early sixties, when he was in college. The clothes fit me fine. I wonder if Eugenia will let me have some of this stuff.

I lounged around the room in my father's old clothes, a pair of tan pants and a lime-green shirt. It makes my eyes look greener, which is probably why he bought it. I was playing out two scenes in my head. In one I am walking into the house in Vicksburg, and Stephanie is running into my arms, laughing and crying at the same time. My mother hovers smiling in the background. Grant has been magically vaporized.

In another scene I am walking into a house I've never seen before, and there is my father, and he sees somebody who looks the way he used to look twenty-seven years ago, wearing his clothes. At first he seems astonished, and then the surprise melts away and I can see that he's glad I'm there.

On the basis of those imaginary scenes I've decided to take some of the clothes. I'm pretty sure Eugenia won't mind. In a way they are already mine; they feel like they belong to me. They certainly aren't doing her any good. I stretched out on my dad's bed in my dad's clothes. The next thing I knew, there was a knock on the door and Tillie's voice, "Breakfast in a half hour, Dennis."

Breakfast was never a big thing back home. It's everybody for himself or herself. Grant is always the first one up, around five-thirty, sitting by himself at the kitchen table with a big bowl of bran or chaff or straw or whatever other indigestible materials he likes to mix with a banana—for potassium—and skim milk so low in fat you can practically see through it. There is a little tray in the middle of the table with a lineup of bottles of all kinds of vitamins and minerals and allergy pills and whatever else he needs to keep his system operating.

He has talked Mother into taking a lot of this stuff, too, especially calcium. She eats so much calcium I'm afraid she'll turn to solid bone. Mother doesn't eat breakfast at all, which drives Grant wild. He says she'd be much healthier if she would begin the day with a solid breakfast, and she would also lose weight. She says nothing but starvation will make her lose weight. Eating food she doesn't want when she doesn't want it will not help, and since she's never sick, why should she worry about getting healthy? Which is true. My mother never catches anything. The whole town can be down with flu, but not Mother.

Stephanie has only liquids for breakfast, strange concoctions mixed from stuff she buys at the health food store. Corky is the only one who packs down a real breakfast. She eats a melted cheese sandwich and a bowl of applesauce every morning of her life, and she would change that to a cheeseburger and applesauce if Grant would let her. Grant is petrified that Corky will grow up to be fat. He's afraid she has inherited Mother's fat genes instead of his thin ones. She has definitely got his poor eyesight. Only six years old and her glasses look about a half-inch thick, almost as thick as his.

Me, I'm just basically lazy. I don't think much about food until around noon, when my body is finally awake, and then I think of it constantly for the next ten or twelve hours. That's like my mother, except she's overweight and I could stand to add another ten pounds.

There is no shower in the bathroom down the hall from my room, from James's room, only a cracked rubber hose with a shower head hooked up to the faucets of the old bathtub. I jackknifed into it and hosed myself down, soaped up, hosed down again. The towels are small and thin with age. I used two and was on the third one before I got reasonably dry. I put back on the same clothes I wore yesterday. My chin felt rough enough for a shave, but there wasn't time.

Tillie and Eugenia were waiting at the polished mahogany table in the dining room. There were three places set, half a grapefruit at each place. I sat down. They smiled and asked how I slept and was the bed all right and so on. Then we began on the grapefruit, which was very sour. I hate sour things. There was no sugar on the table, and since nobody else was using any I had to suffer through. Sugar is a big issue back home. Grant is dead set against sugar. Mother says it is one of the joys of life, and she will not give up drinking it in her coffee or sprinkling it on all sorts of odd things, like tomatoes.

Tillie cleared away the grapefruit halves, theirs neatly emptied, mine mangled, and came back with a tray with three eggs sitting in fancy china egg cups decorated with painted flowers. I had never eaten an egg from an eggcup, so I watched Eugenia. She expertly sliced off the top of the eggshell, sprinkled a few grains of salt into the egg, and ate right down into the shell with a tiny spoon. I tried to do it the same way. Not as neatly as Eugenia, but I managed.

There was a set of silver salt and pepper shakers at each place. Salt is another major issue at home. You can guess who is on which side: Grant anti-salt, Mother pro-salt. Actually I don't think she's really in favor of salt either, but it gives her something safe to disagree about, and it seems people who have been married for a long time need things to argue over.

With the egg came one slice of whole wheat toast cut in triangles. I was dying for a cup of coffee, strong and laced with lots of milk and sugar. "I hope you can forgive a pair of old ladies," Eugenia said, "but there is no coffee. We hope you'll be satisfied with tea." I was not, but I lied and said it was fine.

"Now I'll tell you about Marian Anderson," she said, stirring her tea. "Our mothers grew up together. For years I believed Marian and I were cousins, but we're not actually related." She took a little sip of tea. "Marian was born in 1902, the same year I was, in Philadelphia. She started singing in church choirs there. I remember going with my mother on the train, all the way from Chicago, just to hear her sing. I was so thrilled!

"Then she went to Europe to sing. They didn't want anything to do with her in this country. That was in 1924. I was twenty-two, and her life was so exciting compared to mine! She was the first black to be named a permanent member of the Metropolitan Opera Company—quite an achievement for that time! And she was the first black to perform at the White House.

"But it wasn't always easy, you know. Back in 1939, the Daughters of the American Revolution forbade her to perform at Constitution Hall in Washington. That's when Eleanor Roosevelt resigned her DAR membership in protest. You *do* know who Eleanor Roosevelt was, I hope?" Eugenia demanded suddenly. "You seem not to be terribly well educated, Dennis."

I said I did, but didn't admit exactly how little I knew.

"We went to New York for Marian's debut at the Met, your grandfather and I and everybody else who could get there. We even stayed at the Waldorf-Astoria, which was quite the grand hotel in those days. You should have seen the looks on their faces when a group of black people— Negroes, they used to say—walked in. I was wearing a mink stole, and your grandfather was wearing a Chesterfield. That's a coat with velvet on the collar. And weren't we grand! A few years later Marian was made an alternate delegate to the UN. Quite a distinguished career."

After breakfast and the latest lesson in black history, I told them I was going out to pick up a few things I need for my trip. I didn't tell them I planned to find an Egg McMuffin and some coffee. I got in Mary Plymouth and turned on the ignition. *Grind grind grind*, nothing. It couldn't be the battery or there wouldn't be that grinding. I kept trying and pumping it gas. Still, it wouldn't turn over. By then I had flooded the engine.

Mary is a 1974 Plymouth Duster, one of the last of her

breed. She has only three gears—Grant's new BMW has five—and the shift is on the steering column. I raised the hood and peered into Mary's engine, an engine that loves to gargle gasoline and suck down oil. She is a heavy-duty consumer, which always translates into money.

I have spent many hours of my life hanging over her insides like that, and an equal number of hours flat on my back underneath her, looking up. I have given her a tune-up, replaced filters of gas and air, put in a new fan belt. I bought a grease gun and lubricated her from one end to the other. I have repacked her wheel bearings, adjusted her linkages. And how does she repay all this loving attention and devotion and selfless investment of about half the money I ever brought home from Gochy's? By finding always one more part to go bad.

Carburetor or distributor, I decided from the way she was acting. Since I had just spent hours taking the carburetor apart and putting it back together again, I thought it was probably okay. I got the distributor cap off, and there was a big crack right down the side. I'd have to get to a parts store to buy a new one, and then check the wires. Maybe something had come loose. At least that was no big thing.

I was hanging over Mary's engine when I heard a car pull up across the street, but I didn't pay any attention to it. Then I was aware that somebody was standing right next to me: long brown feet with bright pink toenails and white sandals. Roxanne, come to take me on a tour of the city.

I had not really forgotten about it, but I'm going to

admit right here, right out loud, Doctor Panasonic, that I was scared. Because I had been thinking about her, remembering her huge brown eyes and the way she looked at me. It made me think about things.

When I lay down on that narrow bed last night in my dad's clothes, it wasn't Stephanie I was thinking about. It was Roxanne. Then Stephanie came into my mind, too, and the two of them stayed there: one slim and pale and the other big, with round breasts and rich, dark skin. I wanted them both and they blended into one person, and I went off with that person before I fell asleep.

Roxanne stood looking over my shoulder. She had on a bright green sundress with bare shoulders and a full skirt that swung around her legs. Her white earrings were big as flowers. "Ready?" she asked, grinning at me.

My hands were covered with grease. "I need to wash up."

"You'd better change your shirt, too."

I looked down. There was a big blop of grease on my only decent shirt. "I'll be right back," I said, and ran for the house.

I scrubbed the grease off my hands and examined my filthy shirt. There was a solution—one of James's shirts from the 1960s. I tore off my clothes and pulled on a pair of his pants and one of his open-collared shirts. It looked strange, so out of date, but maybe not really here in Chicago. Couldn't wear this outfit in the Burg. I thought of putting on a necktie, but I didn't know how to tie the knot. Then I went to find Eugenia to tell her I was going out.

But Roxanne was perched on the front porch rail, talking with her.

"Is it all right, Grandmother?" I asked her. "I'll see you later, and we can talk some more."

"Of course it's all right, James," she said. *James*—I didn't know if she knew she had made a mistake or not. Then she laughed. "Listen to me! I know you're Dennis. It's just that you look so much like him." Her laugh turned sad and made me uncomfortable.

I followed Roxanne down the steps to her little Triumph convertible, and I jumped over the door and into the passenger seat. Roxanne did the same on her side in a swirl of skirt.

"Are we ready for this?" she asked, starting the car. It was a great old car, about a '79.

"Yes," I said, "but you need a tuneup. Your idle is really rough."

"Is it?"

Now that is what I consider a crying shame, when somebody has a nice car and doesn't know the first thing about taking care of it. "Yes. You'd be surprised how much better it could run if you'd spend a little time and money on it."

She shrugged. "Maybe so." Then she looked straight at me. "Want to work on it?"

"Yes," I said.

"Good," she said.

I knew I wouldn't be leaving Chicago tomorrow, or maybe even the day after that.

Roxanne is an expert driver. Unlike Stephanie. Stephanie acts as though a car is some foreign object with which she has no relationship. It used to break my heart to ride with her in Grant's BMW, on those rare occasions when he let her drive it and I'd go along.

Chicago traffic is heavy. I'm not used to driving in cities, and I would have been *tense*, at the very least. Roxanne slithered through it with perfect timing. She knew how to run those gears on the TR-7, downshifting smoothly, rarely hitting the brakes. I tried to tell Stephanie about downshifting on the Beamer, but she brushed me off. "I have brakes to slow down," she said, and kept it in high gear even when the engine lugged and pleaded for more power. Finally I gave up. It's her father's car, and if she isn't interested, that's nothing to me.

Roxanne didn't talk much when she was driving, which I liked. She kept her eyes on the road, moving smoothly. The wind whipped her hair. "That's the University of Chicago on your left," she said, pointing to some Gothic buildings with modern ones mixed in. The road wound through a big park with lagoons, and then we came out by the lake. It was a perfect blue, dotted with white sailboats and ruffled with whitecaps. Roxanne headed north, up Lakeshore Drive, Lake Michigan on our right, and I sat back and relaxed and soaked up the sunshine. So this is Chicago, I thought. Chicago, Chicago, dee dee dadadada. . . . And I even stopped being quite so nervous around Roxanne, although I couldn't stop being aware of her.

She swung off the Drive and we entered a large park. Lincoln Park, the sign said. "We're going to the zoo," she announced.

For the rest of the morning we wandered around and stared at the animals. I have always preferred the big cats, which were snoozing in the heat and humidity. We talked about what we would want to be if we could be animals. "You never know," she said. "You might come back as some beast. You ought to be thinking about which one you'd prefer, if you have any choice in the matter."

"Do you really believe that? Reincarnation as a rhinoceros or something?"

"I believe that there are certain lessons we have to learn, and that if we don't learn them the first time through, then maybe we have to come back and do it again until we get it right. It's entirely possible that I might have to live the life of a cheetah or a giraffe and learn whatever lesson there is in that. I think I'd prefer being a giraffe, though, if you make me choose."

"Why a giraffe?"

"They have such an overview of the world, an aerial perspective without ever leaving the ground. And I like to keep my feet on the ground."

"Actually?" I looked at her feet—sexy feet with those white sandals.

"Literally and figuratively."

It was close to noon when we left the zoo. I was starving. I had been starving since breakfast. I thought we might stop by a McDonald's for lunch, but Roxanne had other ideas. "I know a good Chinese restaurant down near the Art Institute, which is our next stop."

Out into traffic again and down Michigan Avenue, past all the expensive stores. Then she swung into a narrow side street and slipped into a parking place. "The one magical gift that I have," she said, "is always being able to find a place to park. They say there is no such thing as parking on the street in Chicago, but I always find a slot right away. In a city like this, that gift is worth money. Now," she said, "do you want to feed your body or your spirit first?"

No contest. Without a well-fed body, my spirit doesn't exist. Roxanne led me to a hole-in-the-wall and explained the mysteries of *dim sum*, a kind of Chinese snack. The waiter, who also seemed to be the cook, came to our table carrying a tray. He smiled without opening his lips and made a little bow to Roxanne, who knew his name.

"I'll do the ordering," she said. "Trust me." She pointed to a couple of little dishes. Wu, I think she called him, set down the tray and arranged little plates in front of us, each with two or three or four strange-looking items. Roxanne unsheathed her chopsticks and transferred a couple of things onto my plate, explaining what was in each—here a little pork something, there a little shrimp something.

"You don't know how to eat with chopsticks? Here, let me show you." She arranged them in my hand and placed my fingers correctly. "Denny, *relax*, will you? They'll break if you clutch them like that." She handled hers like a precision instrument. She ate with chopsticks the same way she drove her car—skillfully, smoothly, without effort. Somehow I managed to get the food into my face and not down the front of my father's 1960s suit and shirt.

Every so often Mr. Wu reappeared with a tray of new items, and Roxanne chose three more: barbecued pork in a soft white dumpling, a pancake with meat and vegetables, a spaghetti salad so spicy it brought tears to my eyes. We sipped strange-tasting tea from little cups without handles.

While we ate Roxanne asked me questions about myself and what I was doing and why. I told her about my father, and why I was looking for him. I told her about my mother and her husband, Dr. Grant, and their little girl, Corky. I described the kind of superkid that Corky is and how she takes care of Shirley the babysitter. I told her about my mother's idea of being the reincarnation of George Sand.

Guess who I did not tell her about.

I didn't know what to do when Mr. Wu put the bill down in front of me, because I was really worried about running out of money. The best I could manage was to pay my half. "Forget it," Roxanne said. "This is on me." I protested, but not very hard. "You can pay the next time," she said. "We'll eat at the Palmer House." I could tell by the name I couldn't afford it, not now, maybe not ever.

Roxanne says the Art Institute is famous all over the world. I don't know much about art, hardly anything at all. Stephanie does, though. When she was living in Philadelphia she used to go to the Philadelphia Art Museum every Saturday. "Remember the scene in *Rocky* when

Sylvester Stallone ran up that big flight of steps?" she asked me once. "That's the Art Museum." And that was all I knew about art, Sylvester Stallone running up the steps of a museum, long before he thought of *Rambo*.

It costs two dollars to get in, if you're a student. Big Spender slapped down a five for two tickets and pocketed the change. All of this seemed to be very amusing to Roxanne. By this time I was so aware of her physical presence I could hardly stand it. It seemed to me I could feel her skin, even though I wasn't touching her. I could smell her hair and her soap. I felt like I was going to choke. I wanted to touch her. She led me through those big white rooms full of fine pictures, and I stared at a painting that she was telling me was by some famous Impressionist painter, and all I could think about was kissing her.

This is not quite the same as the way I feel about Stephanie. Stephanie and I are connected through our souls, and our bodies are just outward shells of the inwardness we share. I don't know anything about Roxanne's inwardness, but I feel as though I know something about every hair on her head, every eyelash, every tooth in her mouth—that I have seen every expression her face has ever shown. I know how Stephanie feels about everything; I can guess what she's thinking and how she will react, because we are that much alike. I have no idea what Roxanne feels or what she thinks, and I don't particularly care.

However, I did wonder if she was thinking about me the way I was thinking about her. Would she be shocked if she could read my mind? That smile, what was behind it? She would probably think I'm ridiculous, falling for her like this. All through the Art Institute I was trying to brush her hand accidentally, bumping up against her, managing to stand close behind her when she was talking about a picture so that her hair would touch my face. Now this is stupid, I said to myself. She is six years older than I am. She probably thinks I'm a dumb kid. It probably amuses her to watch me getting hot and bothered.

She would watch me with that wise smile and then slip out of reach, leaving me standing there grabbing at empty air, and she wouldn't be smiling, she'd be laughing. I couldn't blame her.

I don't remember one picture from the Art Institute. The huge sculpture of Adam, that registered, but I was thinking more about the Eve beside me. I couldn't come up with a sane response to any of the things she was telling me. Finally she turned and looked straight at me. She's very tall. "I don't think you're much interested in this. Let's go do something else."

We walked back to her car in silence.

"Do you have a girlfriend?" she asked me when we were moving again.

"No." That quick I said it, without even pausing. But as soon as it was out of my mouth I wanted to call it back. Oh, Stephanie! I really didn't mean that!

"No? Hard to believe, Denny, a dynamite guy like you. Or are you into numbers? Too many to keep track of?"

"Actually I do have somebody I like. But she's back there—"

"And I'm here," Roxanne said, looking at me with her head cocked to one side and that odd smile.

I just nodded. Couldn't say anything.

"How long are you going to stay around Chicago?"

"I don't know. A few days. I want to work on my car."

"And mine, too? You promised."

"Yes."

"Then where will you go?"

"To see my other grandmother in Nebraska. And then to San Francisco to see my father."

"Driving across the country alone. It's a rite of passage. I drove to New Orleans when I was eighteen. Everybody needs to do something like that." She reached over and took my hand. "How long here then?"

I swallowed hard. "Two more days. Maybe three."

"Then let's not waste them," she said, and held my hand against her cheek. I stopped breathing.

I should have asked her if she has a boyfriend, and if not, why not. It is hard to believe that a beautiful twenty-four-year-old woman would be attracted to an eighteen-year-old guy, especially a tall, skinny one with a beat-up old car and no money, who is running headlong toward both past and future. But I didn't think about that.

I told her I'd eat dinner with Grandmother and Tillie, and after they went to bed, I'd come out on the porch and wait for her.

She'll be here in three more hours.

Tape 6

Friday, July 11th, on the road in Illinois.

I have not talked to this machine for ten days. No time to talk, hardly any time to think since the night Roxanne came back for me.

Tillie and Grandmother Eugenia were waiting for me in the dining room that evening. The table was set with a lace cloth and napkins and water goblets and extra spoons and forks. There was one miniature lamb chop for each of us, two tiny boiled potatoes, a spoonful of peas, and a microscopic salad with one cherry tomato. "We made an extra potato for you," Tillie said. "I notice you have a big appetite."

Eugenia had decided this was the night to talk about black writers and poets. Langston Hughes, it turns out, was another of her old buddies. "I won't ask if you've heard of him," she said. "He lived in France and Mexico for a while, one more black man who couldn't find acceptance in his own country."

So why, knowing all these people, couldn't Eugenia understand that my father had to go to Paris? Why was she still holding this against him? Anyway, somebody discovered Langston Hughes's poetry when he was about twenty-three, and a book of his poems was published and earned him enough money to go to college.

"Langston was very much involved in the Harlem Renaissance," Eugenia informed me.

I ate the lamb chop in two bites and tried to listen to the lecture, which would have been interesting if I hadn't been thinking *Stephanie/Roxanne/Steffy/Roxy.* "Back in the 1920s Langston and Countee Cullen—that's another black writer—used to gather at the library in Harlem with other poets and talk and talk and talk. Langston told us about those get-togethers. Cullen was the same age as Langston, and he went on to get a master's degree from Harvard."

I swallowed the potatoes and salad in a couple more bites.

"Now," Eugenia said, "what about you, Dennis? I just go on and on and on about things you probably have no interest in, and I haven't given you a minute to talk about yourself."

"But I'm really interested in the things you're telling me, Grandmother," I said, feeling suddenly on the spot. "I like learning all this stuff. Maybe I'll even read some of that poetry. I've been listening to your records of Paul Robeson and Marian Anderson, and they're absolutely great. I know a lot about jazz musicians, but I don't know anything about the serious stuff. Gospel music, too—I want to learn about that."

"I'm glad to hear you're interested, Dennis, but that does nothing to change the fact that I'm interested in *you*. After all, you're my grandson—my only grandson, did you know that? And it's time for us to get acquainted."

But I was thinking, Yeah, this is great, but Roxanne is coming to pick me up after a while, and I'm getting acquainted with her, too. She also wants to know all about me, but I'm betting not the same things Eugenia wants to know.

After dinner Eugenia led the way to the front room, to the grand piano near the window. She carefully folded back the cover over the keys and sat down. "Come sit beside me, Dennis," she said. It was more of an order than an invitation. She played a few chords. It must be very hard for her with her hands all crippled up like that, but even with the gnarled fingers she could play.

"I started each of my boys at the piano when they were just little bits of things," she said, "showing them chords and scales and teaching them to read music. And every one of them put up with that and learned to play little songs and so forth, wriggling around because they wanted to go outside and play ball or ride their bicycles. Except your father. He never had to be reminded to practice. You had to chase him away. For him it wasn't practicing, it was fun. And the talent that boy had!" I thought she was going to cry, but she didn't. "Well, now," she said, "show me what you know. Can you read music?"

"No, ma'am, I can't."

"Your mother never sent you for piano lessons?" she demanded.

"She did, but I never wanted to practice. So she returned the piano. It was rented. I wish we had one, because I like to, you know, fool around."

"Show me how you fool around, Dennis."

Oh, boy. So I played a melody, some stupid thing from a TV commercial. I played that with one hand, and then I did some improvising around it, modulated into another key, wove another theme into it. Then I had another tune that I liked, and I had worked out how to play the two together, weaving one in and out of the other. It was kind of fun. I hadn't done this since I was at Keith's, which seemed like a million years ago, so it was rough at first, but then it started coming back to me, and I really got into it.

Grandmother said, "Dennis, it is a crime that you are not taking lessons. A crime! That was a canon and fugue that you just played, and you don't even know it. It's the kind of music Bach wrote; he was the master of the form. A number of later composers used the same technique: Mozart, for instance, Haydn, Beethoven, Brahms. Do any of those names mean anything to you? Not even Bach?"

"I've heard of them," I said.

"Play some more," she commanded.

"I don't know what you want me to play."

"Improvise."

"On what?"

"Well, this then."

She played some little tune. It sounded vaguely familiar. I repeated it after her, getting it almost right. Played it a second time, working a couple of chords around it, kept playing it, building more and more onto it each time I did. Moved it up into another key—I don't know what key, I never thought of them by name. Then I modulated into a minor, the music that makes you think of funerals and solemn occasions. I took the melody into the bass and wove another line with my right hand.

When I stopped, Eugenia was smiling and shaking her head. "Now try this."

I repeated what she played and began working on variations the way I did before, but I changed the tempo, teased it into jazz rhythms. And guess what—Eugenia started improvising with me, and the next thing I knew I was jamming with my own grandmother and had forgotten everything else. Eugenia said, "If you stay, I'll teach you. You'll have to practice, hours and hours a day, but you'll learn fast. You have all the talent. I can teach you to read music. That's a form of illiteracy that is easily cured. I can make you a pianist. Not like your father, you're not at all like James, but you can *play*."

I didn't know what to say. Then we both spotted Roxanne standing on the porch in the shadows, listening to us.

"Bravo," she said. "Twice bravo."

White pants that fit like skin, a ballooning black shirt tied with a green silk belt, long dangling green earrings that flashed when she moved. I said good night to Eugenia and climbed into the TR-7. Roxanne pulled quickly away and headed into the warm, damp night. "I didn't know you were a pianist," she said.

"I'm not."

"That's not what I heard. I also heard Eugenia offer to teach you if you'd stay. Are you going to take her up on it?"

"I don't know. I never thought of it."

"You're thinking of it now."

"Yes."

"Have you eaten?"

"Sort of. One lamb chop and six peas. They eat like sparrows."

"I'll fix that. I'm taking you to my place," she said. "I hope that's okay."

"It's okay," I said. But suddenly my stomach had tied itself into a strange knot. For the next fifteen minutes or so she maneuvered through the heavy city traffic without talking. I didn't know where I was, had no sense of direction at all. We pulled up in front of an old house.

"I live here," she said, "and you have just had another demonstration of my one and only magical gift."

"Finding parking places?"

"Yes."

Her one-room apartment was in the back, facing a little garden. It was stylish, like Roxanne. Almost everything in the room was white. The floor was painted white, the walls were white, the posters on the wall were mostly white with only dashes of color. There was a mattress on the floor, covered in something that looked like a white rug, and sheets were draped above it to form a sort of canopy. There was a canvas beach chair, white, a table and chairs painted white, and the table was set with white dishes and white napkins and a bunch of white daisies in a glass vase. The effect was startling.

She was watching for my reaction. "Well?"

"Very unusual. I guess you like white."

"Sure. Know why?"

I shrugged.

"It makes everything else stand out. Me, for instance. Don't you agree?"

I couldn't disagree. You certainly did notice her, but you'd notice Roxanne whether she had a white background or not.

"What are we going to eat? Milk and mashed potatoes and vanilla ice cream?"

She gave me a funny look. "Really hungry, are you?"

Really uncomfortable, to tell the truth. I was hungry, but I was also feeling very strange here with her. It was okay when we were roaring around Chicago—museum, zoo, Chinese restaurant—but there was something weird about being here in her place.

She got busy over in the corner in kind of a makeshift kitchen: a small sink and stove and a little refrigerator that fit under the counter, all behind a curtain—white, naturally—that she pushed aside. "Since you're in Chicago on a cultural expedition, I decided to do what I could about that. You're having soul food: collard greens, ham hocks, and corn bread to soak up the pot liquor."

It sounded bad. It looked bad. It tasted . . . bad. I did my best, but I've never liked spinach or any of that stuff. The corn bread was okay—I ate almost all of it. Roxanne watched me. I felt as though I had just failed a test. "I guess I'm not as hungry as I thought I was."

"I don't think that's it at all. I think you're just a bad-ass nigger."

That caught my attention. Did she say what I thought she said? She was grinning. Roxanne has one wicked grin. Then she put on a record. "Billie Holliday," she said. "Blues singer."

"I know who Billie Holliday is," I said. People were acting as though I didn't know one thing about anything, and it was beginning to get me mad.

I was on my feet and pacing around the little apartment. "Look, Roxanne," I said, "there's lots I don't know. I don't know my father, for one thing. I haven't seen him for a long time. That's where I'm going now. I don't know this part of my family. That's why I came here, so I could get to know Eugenia. I don't know much about black history, but then I don't know much about white history. I can't name a half-dozen black poets, but I can't name a half-dozen white poets either. One of these days I'll catch up. But this doesn't mean I don't know I'm black, and it doesn't mean I don't have a good idea of what happens to black people in this country. I remember the first time some punk kid called me a nigger in school and the kind of trouble I got into when I tried to clean up the playground with his face. So I don't need you feeding me greens and calling me a bad-ass nigger to educate me to something you think I don't know about. My mother raised me to be a person, not somebody of one particular color. She raised me to be a *man*, Roxanne, and I can find out about the rest on my own."

She leaned back and looked up at me lazily. "I know very well that your mama raised you to be a man, Denny. Why else would I have brought you here?"

Before she drove me back to Eugenia's late that night she said, "I hope you decide to stay for a while. Take Eugenia up on her offer to teach you. I'll make sure you don't starve. And I promise, no more greens." She leaned over and kissed me. I got out of the car and watched her drive away.

Is it possible to love two people? Now this is something I never thought about before. Guys back in the Burg used to be into multiples, into scoring, into having a bunch of different ladies. I did that myself, a few times. But I didn't think about love. I didn't love them. They were nice and pretty and whatever, and I liked them, but I didn't think about love until Stephanie. Everything I know about love I learned from Stephanie, and what I feel for her is so intense that I can't imagine feeling that way about anyone else, certainly not at the same time. What is it that I feel for Roxanne?

Lust, my mother would say. I heard her say about a friend of hers, Diane, "She's in lust again," meaning she had just found some new guy to get excited about. But the guy never stayed around long, and a few weeks later there would be another one and Mother would say, "Diane's in lust again."

Maybe that's what it is with Roxanne. She's like Stephanie in some ways but completely unlike her in others. For one thing, she's older. Stephanie is sixteen, Roxanne is twenty-four. That's eight years, which makes a lot of difference in a person our age. It's the difference between a girl and a woman. Roxanne is very experienced. She knows things I've hardly ever thought about.

Roxanne is beautiful, but so is Stephanie, only beautiful in a different way. Stephanie is thin, fragile-looking, with pale, pale skin, and sometimes I'm afraid she'll crack, like a china cup. Roxanne is big all over, but not fat. Her shoulders are wide, her legs are strong, and she has big muscular thighs and a broad rear. Her arms are thick and strong, too. *Big* breasts. Her skin is dark, like milk chocolate, like coffee with only a little cream, much darker than mine. Her hair is thick and black and wild as a bush. And she has a way of drooping her eyelids that makes her look as though she knows a secret that is very amusing and has something to do with me.

So I hung around Chicago for over a week, a lot longer than I thought I would. Eugenia had a fit that I was outside every morning working on my car and then on Roxanne's. She would sit up on the porch and watch me down on the street, taking them apart, putting them back together again.

Then I'd come up with grease all over my hands, and she'd *tsk tsk* about that.

"You'll injure your hands," she said, and I said I didn't think so, and explained that I had to take off the wheels and repack the bearings and work on the brakes in order to drive it safely.

"You should be spending this time at the piano," she said.

"But I have to make sure my car is safe," I told her.

She gave me a key so I could come and go when I wanted to. The key ring had a tiny toy piano on it. "It was your father's," she said.

Then, after lunch, with just enough food to ward off starvation, I'd sit at the piano with her, and she'd teach me music theory, explaining key signatures, sharps and flats, majors and minors, and showing me basic chords. I already knew those chords, but I didn't know their names, like A-flat major and so on, and I didn't know that lowering the middle note of a major chord by a half step changed it to a minor, although I knew that instinctively. Then there was the IV chord and the V-7.

Eugenia showed me how to go through all the majors and minors, playing a pattern of chords. This was much more interesting than my piano lessons were a long time ago, when I had to do scales and exercises and didn't really know what they were all about.

She showed me a book on how to match what my hands were doing to what the notes in the book said, how to count the beat—which I already knew instinctively—and how to read a simple line. Then she'd go upstairs and take a nap, and when she came down again I was supposed to demonstrate what I had learned.

What I really loved was when, after a few days, I got to the point where I could read a simple line of music and improvise around it. Eugenia would sit down with me and add her part. Suddenly she'd say something like "key of E!" and I'd know what she was talking about and be able to change what I was playing to that key. She showed me how to do arpeggios, which are just chords that have been broken up into single notes played one at a time.

I wanted to be able to try the complicated pieces in the books of Mozart and Beethoven, the kind James used to play. But we both knew that I was not James and would never be able to play real classical music.

Sometimes I listened to Marian Anderson, and when I thought I had one of her songs in my head, I picked it out on the keyboard: "Swing low, sweet chariot, Comin' for to carry me home. . . ." Key of F, starting out on a IV/ chord, and off I'd go with it, getting into the verse: "I looked over Jordan and what did I see,/Comin' for to carry me home./A band of angels comin' after me,/Comin' for to carry me home."

I was concentrating on that when I looked up, and there was Tillie at the other end of the piano, hands folded under her chin, eyes closed as though she really could see over Jordan, but I didn't know what Jordan was.

Tears were running down the creases in her ancient face.

I kept on playing. When I stopped she opened her eyes and looked at me and smiled. "Thank you, Dennis. Eugenia doesn't care much for spirituals, but I do."

So there was practicing, and playing, and listening to records, and then we'd sit down to a dainty old ladies' supper, a tiny steak or chop or half a chicken breast, a mouthful of rice or potatoes, a bite of fruit for dessert. I had checked the refrigerator and pantry, and there wasn't anything there to munch on. Maybe when you get old, you don't need as much food.

Then, about nine o'clock, I'd say good night and the two old ladies would go off upstairs together, and I'd go sit on the front porch in the muggy June night and wait for the little red Triumph to pull up.

After the first night there were no more collard greens and corn bread, no more soul food. Instead there were all sorts of unusual things, things I can't remember the names of, that she invented for her cooking classes: chicken breasts in curried cream and chutney, black pepper pasta with roasted red and yellow peppers, steak with African spices. Exotic stuff but good, and she always made plenty.

Then Roxanne would say, "Want some dessert, Denny?" and I always did. "Dessert" was the same kind of code word that "Philadelphia" was with Stephanie. I guess people always have some kind of code or signal. So then there would be dessert, as delicious as her cooking, and afterward we'd play some kind of game—she was crazy about games, and she taught me how to play poker, which I won, and Trivial Pursuit, which she won because I didn't seem to know anything at all. And then she'd take me back to Eugenia's.

The days sort of melted into one another. I wasn't keeping track. The cars got fixed, I learned some music, Eugenia lectured me about black culture and black history. She'd recite Langston Hughes's poetry at the dinner table. "He was seventeen, just your age, when he wrote this, Dennis."

When Susanna Jones wears red
Her face is like an ancient cameo
Turned brown by the ages.
Come with a blast of trumpets.
    Jesus!

When Susanna Jones wears red
A queen from some time-dead Egyptian night
Walks once again.
Blow trumpets. Jesus!

And the beauty of Susanna Jones in red
Burns in my heart a love-fire sharp like pain.

Sweet silver trumpets.
    Jesus!

"He had an awful life, poor soul," Eugenia said. "Never had a dime. His father was a successful businessman in Mexico, and he never gave Langston one cent, not one red cent. Instead he left it all to three old women when he died.

Meanwhile Langston was taking care of his crazy mother, spending everything he had on her.

"I got to know him when he was living here, working on his autobiography. Most of the time he was moving around. He said life got too complicated if he ever stayed anywhere for more than six months. He always stopped in to say hello when he was in town after that. He was much taken by your father. I blame Langston for talking James into going to Paris, because that's what *he* did. Always on the move after that, just like James. Just like James." She sounded so sad it would break your heart.

I learned a poem he wrote called "Ardella" and recited it one night to Roxanne.

> I would liken you
> To a night without stars
> Were it not for your eyes.
> I would liken you
> To a sleep without dreams
> Were it not for your songs.

"Denny, nobody has ever recited poetry for me before."

"There's a first time for everything," was my clever reply.

I didn't know exactly what the poems meant. I didn't understand what silver trumpets and Jesus had to do with Susannah Jones, and I was surprised that Grandmother was reciting a poem with Jesus in it because she claimed not to have much to do with Jesus. She rejected him because he let black people suffer, she said. That was why she scorned spirituals, too, because they kept people tied to the idea that there was a Jesus who cared and a place where things were going to be better some day. "We only have the here and now, Dennis," she said. "Make use of it."

I didn't understand the silver trumpets, but I knew what the line meant, "Burns in my heart a love-fire sharp like pain." The beauty of Roxanne was burning a love-fire of some kind in my heart, and it was sharp like pain. She was driving me crazy. She was like a tick, getting under my skin, and she knew it. She enjoyed it. I could tell that she knew she had gotten to me, and she was loving it.

I had been in Chicago for about a week when a letter arrived from Stephanie.

Roxanne had just dropped me off, around midnight. I was thinking about Stephanie, beginning to understand that I might not see her for a long time, and that when I did, our lives would be changed and we would be completely different people. We are both young, I said to myself, sounding in my head like my own mother; we need to meet other people, find out about the world. The interesting thing is that I didn't believe that when I was with her in Vicksburg; I didn't believe that when I was driving along I-80 in the rain. It was an idea that only made good sense to me after I met Roxanne.

Something was lying on my pillow. I must not have noticed it earlier. A letter, addressed to me, in care of Mrs. Eugenia Brown. Return address, S.L.W., Vicksburg, PA. I ripped open the envelope, nearly demolishing it. Pale blue notepaper with STEPHANIE printed in square red letters across the top and her loopy handwriting:

"Dearest Denny," it said, "I hope this reaches you. I don't know how much longer I will be here. Daddy is still upset about what happened, and he says that I have to go away to boarding school in Philadelphia this year. It's that or back to the castle. Mom and I have been talking, but I'm not sure how well it would work for us to try to live together again. Daddy's insisting that I go to a girls' school. I'll probably have to wear a veil and not be allowed to have another date until I'm twenty-five and then only with two chaperones present. Your mother is trying to talk some sense into him. It isn't working. He says she wouldn't be so blasé (sp?) if it were her daughter. Whichever way it goes, though, I won't be here when you get back, whenever that is.

"The only real friend I have is Corky. She told me she saw you in your mom's study, with her address book. And she told me that you called long distance. She's so smart, that kid! She snuck the address book out, and we went through it together, and she said, 'I bet this is what he's going to do—go visit his grandma.' Can you imagine that? We agreed that we wouldn't tell your mom what we came up with, unless it seemed like an emergency.

"Maybe you could write to me at Gochy's, and I'll go out there in a few days and see if there's a letter

back from you. I was pretty embarrassed, but I called and told him you might be writing to me, and would he keep it a secret, and he said yes, he'd do that if I'd pass on the message to you that there's a job here for you when you come back, and he hopes it's a good trip.

"Oh, Denny, I love you so much and I miss you so much and I don't know how this is all going to work out. Sometimes I'm afraid it won't. I'm scared that I'll never see you again. And it all seems so unfair. You've only been gone for a week, and it's like my life has ended. I just don't feel like eating or doing anything. Daddy says if I don't eat he'll put me in the hospital and feed me intravenously. I yelled at him and told him it's his fault that I'm too miserable to eat.

"Maybe you don't want to answer this letter. Maybe you don't love me anymore. Maybe you hate me. Sometimes I think if you loved me you wouldn't have left, no matter what my father said to you. We could have faced it together. Your mom blames me because you left. She says it's my fault, that I should have had more sense than to get involved with you, knowing how Daddy would react. But I didn't know it would turn out like this.

"Oh, Denny I do love you so much!"

Then there was a row of **XOXOXOX**, kisses and hugs, and her signature.

Talk about feeling *confused*! Everything came apart for

me when I read Steffy's letter. There had been security in knowing Stephanie was back in the Burg, guarded by a dragon, but *there*. *I* was the one on the move, *I* was the one searching things out, she was staying in one place, and we'd work it out somehow. But now that isn't the way it's going to be. She's going back to Philadelphia.

I decided it was time to leave Chicago. I packed up and got ready to leave. I explained to Eugenia at breakfast that I had to move on, to find my father. I asked her if I could take his clothes, and she said yes. She said I should keep the house key with the little piano in case I came back. I promised it would be soon. She cried a little, and Tillie cried, too, and went to the kitchen to fix me tiny sandwiches with the crusts trimmed off for my trip.

Roxanne's beauty is burned in my heart, and it will stay there. But it's Stephanie I love, and I had to go. I was too much of a coward to say good-bye to Roxanne. I wouldn't have wanted to leave. I might have changed my mind again.

And so I left early this morning, and now here I am again, out on I-80 West. Soon I'll be in Iowa.

Tape 7

Saturday, July 12th, Davenport, Iowa.

The more space I put between me and Chicago, me and Roxanne, the better I feel. Crossing the Mississippi was exciting, a kind of symbolic act. I didn't want to cruise over it on the interstate—it needed a ceremony—and so I bailed off I-80 and circled around Rock Island, in Illinois, and found the Centennial Bridge, which goes from Rock Island to Davenport. So there it was, the Mighty Miss.

I started bellowing, "Ol' man river, dat ol' man river," trying to sound like Paul Robeson, except I'm no bass, no singer at all, and it must have sounded really stupid. But I did it anyway.

And now I am in Iowa. So far it has been Pennsylvania, Ohio, Indiana, Illinois, and now Iowa, State Number Five. I followed signs to the Village of East Davenport, one of those historical areas with brick streets, built right on the bluff overlooking the Mississippi. I wandered around there for a long time, staring out at the river. There's something about rivers that I really like. Grant used to say that someday we'd go canoeing on the Susquehanna and camp out along the way, maybe go all the way down to where it flows into Chesapeake Bay.

Naturally we never went.

I say "naturally" because I found out there are two kinds of people in the world, people who do what they say they're going to do and people who don't. If Grant swears that he will do something, taking an oath, which he did with Stephanie on the matter of the dancing lessons, then he keeps his word, because you can always go back to him and say, "Grant, on such-and-such a day you promised to do such-and-such." And that works.

What doesn't work is if he's talking idly about what he's going to do someday. That never happens, but you go around half hoping it *will* happen, even though you know it won't. He was always talking about fixing up the house, remodeling my room and putting a bathroom on the third floor, but he never did. That used to make Mother mad. He said when they got married that they would completely redecorate the house, because she said she didn't want to live with some other woman's taste, and about once a year she'd bring up the subject again, and he'd have some excellent reason for not doing it then. He'd say, "We'll see." That infuriated her.

That canoe trip down the Susquehanna was one of those deals. Not that I was so excited about it, because I couldn't quite see Dr. Grant and me paddling away, day after day, and setting up a camp at night and cooking over a camp- fire and telling stories. Grant likes to think of himself as an outdoorsman. He's on the mailing list for L.L. Bean and Eddie Bauer, and he orders all kinds of Maine Hunting Shoes and wool flannel shirts and mountain parkas, which he wears around the Burg as though he's about to leave on a hunting and fishing expedition as soon as his last patient either recovers or dies.

But he never goes anywhere, although he certainly looks ready for action. Every time a new catalog arrives, he gets excited and sits at the kitchen table making a list of the things he wants: a fly rod, a special vest for holding photographic equipment, a backpacking tent suitable for Arctic expeditions. Once he actually got around to ordering a pair of snowshoes, but I'm absolutely positive they have not been in contact with snow. He tries to convince my mother to order some gear as well, so the two of them can stomp off into the wilderness together. She just laughs and says she hates the woods, she's not into field-and-stream, and please not to bring home any fish to be gutted or pheasants to be plucked.

That reminds me of the time last fall when a pheasant flew smack into their bedroom window and killed itself. We heard the noise and all ran out to the yard to see what had happened, and there it lay, still fluttering a little. Then it stopped fluttering. "Dead," Corky pronounced, like a coroner. She described how it had come swooping up out of the high grass in the field behind the house and, *bam*, against the window. Any other kid her age probably would have been in tears, or at least planning a funeral for the poor dead bird, but Corky thought we ought to eat it. How many times does a pheasant drop into your yard? she wanted to know.

Grant was elected to clean it, since he's the doctor, but if you can believe this, it was actually Corky who did it. Grant told her what to do, and she did it. This was the phase when she decided she would be a world-famous heart surgeon when she grew up. She was five then and not in the least bit afraid of blood and guts. Stephanie wouldn't even look at the bird, and when Mother served it up with wild rice that night, Stephanie refused to come to the table. Corky dived right in.

I got very homesick, sitting up there on the bluff above the river and thinking about Corky and Mother and Stephanie. I wondered what they were all doing at that moment, while I was watching the Mississippi. I should send some postcards, in addition to the letter I'm going to write to Stephanie.

I was even beginning to be lonesome for Grant, who, to tell the truth, is not really that bad a person most of the time. We have our differences, for sure, but I guess that's true of everybody. And we never actually fought about anything, until that business with Stephanie, and now that I look back at it, I guess if it was my daughter I'd do the same thing. I mean, Stephanie is only sixteen, and fathers still look after their daughters at that age.

The river is a symbol of being cut off from another part of the country and another life. It divides me from Stephanie and my mother and the rest of the family. It also separates me from Roxanne. All of that was more than

I could handle. Roxanne and I never talked about families and things like that. It was as if we didn't have any past, or any future either. Stephanie and I know everything about each other's past; it can be uncomfortable sometimes, to have somebody know you that well.

None of that with Roxanne. I asked her about her folks, and she made a joke and brushed it off. I don't even know if she has brothers and sisters. Or boyfriends. I asked her if she had one, because she was spending a lot of time with me, and she had asked me about girls. She shrugged and smiled and said, "I know a lot of guys," in a way that told me it was none of my business. Her life is all white space, like her apartment, so that the only thing that stands out is her.

It was a case of being attracted against my will, almost as though I had nothing to say about what happened, as though what happened was *destined* to happen. I do not like that feeling, of not being in control. Today by the river, eating Tillie's doll-sized sandwiches, which disappeared in a second because I was starving, I knew that if I had stayed in Chicago any longer, maybe even one more day, I would have been lost.

There I was, on the banks of the Mississippi, a knight on a quest, an explorer in search of a new continent, and I kept going back to Roxanne. And to Stephanie. *Roxanne/ Stephanie/Stephanie/Roxanne.* Well, enough of that. I jumped up and made sure there was nobody around, and yelled, "It's me! It's Dennis James Brown!" I sat down again and felt kind of stupid.

Then I began thinking ahead to my next destination: Grandma Sunderland's, on the other end of Nebraska, about six hundred miles to go.

Mary cruised along today with no problem. It's a boring drive. Everything is big—fields as far as you can see. It's flat, nothing much to look at, a big change for a kid from Pennsylvania used to hills and little farms with small houses and a few horses out in the fields. Around Vicksburg, Amish buggies clip-clop slowly along country roads.

Every Wednesday Mother goes to Farmer's Market and comes home with a pie or cake or sticky buns that she buys from one of the Amish ladies. She even found out their names and where they live, how many kids they have and so on. We'd be eating the shoofly pie or the upside down cake—that is, Mother and Corky and I would be, and the other two would be nibbling three crumbs apiece—and she'd bring us up to date on the latest on Hannah Stoltzfus and her family. My mother is like that, always wanting to know about people's lives. Grant says she is the most curious woman he has ever met, and her curiosity is going to get her into trouble.

Grant is curious, too, but about scientific stuff. They subscribe to *Scientific American*, and Grant reads the articles about hard science and Mother reads the ones about people. She has fantasies about going off to live in some remote place, among the Eskimos in Alaska, for instance, and getting to know their culture. That is in the same category as her fantasy of traveling around France, retracing the steps of her heroine, George Sand.

My question is: why does a person like my mother marry a person like Grant West? And vice versa? More important, why did a person like my mother marry a person like my father, who then leaves? And then what happens? To the son, for instance? When I know the answers to those questions, I will have the secret of the universe.

Meanwhile, a problem I don't want to think about. When I stopped for gas this morning, I bought an ice cream bar and made the mistake of biting on it on the right side of my mouth, the side with the tooth with the hole in it. Thought I'd go through the roof for a minute or two.

Sunday, July 13th. Nebraska, somewhere.

Last night, after I sat around for a while being philosophical by the banks of the Mississippi, I found a place to put up my tent and settled down. It was hot, and there seemed to be an army of mosquitoes in search of dinner. They ate better than I did; all I had had were the last of Tillie's one-bite sandwiches. First I couldn't get to sleep, then nothing but crazy dreams all night long, tossing and turning and swatting mosquitoes. My tooth was throbbing. I was more tired this morning when I got up than I was when I went to bed. Sunrise comes very early out here in the flatlands with no hills to block it.

I worry about Mary Plymouth, the only female in my life right now. She had better be faithful and true and keep me going. The brakes definitely feel better, but I keep my eye on the temperature gauge. Every couple of hours I ease into a gas station, check the water, add a little if it needs it, look at the tires. And worry. If I had known I was going to drive across the country, I would have bought her a new set of shoes before we left, because these are definitely worn. But I don't have the money, and all I can do is keep my fingers crossed. The money situation is tight, but I should make it okay if there are no emergencies.

Through Iowa City, then Des Moines. When it was still early, I pulled in at a truck stop and gassed up. I went into the café and sat down at the counter next to a row of truckers, all of them joking with the waitress, who sped up and down the counter, sloshing coffee into a row of mugs. She had a face that looks as though her feet hurt. Every now and then she stopped and dragged on a cigarette that she keeps next to the hot chocolate machine.

I ordered eggs over easy and home fries and toast and coffee, but it came with applesauce and sausages, too. I told her that I didn't order sausages. "You look like you need them," she said. "I won't charge you for them, just enjoy them." So I did.

I wondered where all those guys were going. What a life that must be, driving big trucks hour after hour, day after day. If I were more like my mother, I'd start a conversation with one of them and find out what it's like.

I didn't go into Des Moines but kept right on. One hundred twenty-three miles later, another two hours and something, and I was skirting Council Bluffs, which is in Iowa, and crossing the border into Nebraska. There's another river here, the Missouri. "Across the wide Missouri!" I bellowed, driving over the bridge. I don't know how I know that song. Maybe from my mother, who was a child of the sixties and knows all kinds of folk songs.

Nebraska is flat, flat, flat. I saw signs for Lincoln, the state capital, and decided to get off there and follow the Cornhusker Highway into town. Driving in strange cities makes me nervous, but it was Sunday and very quiet. I drove by the capitol building, which has a big gold statue on top. I parked the car and walked around a little, thinking, Well, golly, Denny, here you are in Lincoln, Nebraska. How about that? Then I tried to find a coffee shop to take on some more caffeine, which I seem to need a lot of when I'm behind the wheel, but everything was closed.

So I crawled back in Mary Plymouth, which was incredibly hot, and started out again, windows open, air howling in my ears, trucks roaring by. The map showed a road, just a black line running parallel to I-80. That's what I wanted. I got out of Lincoln and onto that two-lane road.

I listened to the radio, twirling the dial to catch the local stations to find out what was going on. Lots of religious programs out here. I kept twirling. Every four or five miles there was another little town. I made a game of trying to remember the names. Seward. Then Tamora; Seward and Tamora. Next Utica; Seward, Tamora, Utica. Waco. But then I had already forgotten Tamora and I gave up the game. What would it be like to live in one of these little towns? What do people do with themselves in Waco, Nebraska?

Then I got to a place called North Platte, which is the home of Buffalo Bill, and they don't let you forget it. I had no idea who Buffalo Bill was, but it wasn't too hard to find out, because everything in that town has something to do with him. It turns out his real name was William Frederick Cody, and he was a scout and a buffalo hunter who eventually got into show business. In 1883 he organized Buffalo Bill's Wild West Show and toured all over America and Europe with it for years and years. I guess he had a lot of adventures—hunting buffalo and riding for the Pony Express and things like that.

What really interested me about Buffalo Bill, more than all the wild adventures, which were probably partly made up and partly exaggerated, was that he was a *kid* when he started doing all that. His father died when he was eleven years old, and he had to support the family. He was only thirteen when he worked in the Colorado goldfields and fourteen when he was a Pony Express rider. I am almost eighteen and I haven't really done anything at all. I'm driving Mary across the country, but Bill Cody was a lot younger than I am and he was galloping through dangerous Indian territory. At times like this I feel as though I live a very dull life.

Then I drove south a ways and found a little campground that doesn't charge anything at all, hardly any RVs, nothing fancy, but there is a lake for swimming. It seems like a good place to stop and think about how I am going to get in touch with Grandma Sunderland. I try to tell myself that it worked out okay with Eugenia, that Eugenia and I got along fine and I learned a lot from her, and it will be fine with Grandma Sunderland, too.

I put on some shorts that pass for a swimming suit and jumped in. Then I figured, now that I had worked some of Roxanne out of my blood, I could write some reasonable kind of letter to Stephanie.

When Stephanie first arrived in the Burg she was still in love with that rich guy from Philadelphia, a Jewish kid her mother couldn't stand. After Christmas, when we found each other, she wanted to write and tell Bart she wasn't going to be involved with him anymore, but I talked her into not doing it.

"We need a cover," I said. "Bart Schwartz is as good a cover as any. And he's at a safe distance."

Stephanie let me read her letters to Bart after that. She claims she is not a writer; all of her intellect is in her body. The letter she sent me showed how wrong she was. But writing letters to Bozo Bart was really hard for her. He plans to be a novelist, in addition to an international lawyer, and he used to write tremendously long letters, telling her everything he had said and done and thought for the past couple of weeks. She read them to me. They were massively boring. He had a lot to learn if he was going to be a novelist. Little did he know that a good plot was developing around him at that very moment.

"Did you ever make love to him?" I asked her once, afraid of what her answer was going to be, but there wasn't any way I could keep from asking.

"That's a private matter," she said, but then she put her arms around me and kissed me and said, "I've never loved anybody but you."

Whether she did or not, and sometimes I thought one way and sometimes the other, it was Bart's letters that caused the final blow-up with the dragon and Stephanie's banishment to the Burg. Her mother found some of the letters and read them. And whether they had ever had sex or not, Bart certainly thought a lot about it and described in detail exactly what he would like to do to her, as often as possible.

Stephanie and her mother had a huge fight. Stephanie said her mail was private and her mother had no right to come into her room, go through her desk, open her letters, and read them. The dragon argued that it was her job to protect Stephanie, to guard her morals, and that it was therefore her right to take whatever measures were required, including listening in on telephone conversations and reading mail.

Amazingly, Grant sided with Stephanie, claiming she had a right to privacy. This, of course, has its humorous side, because when it comes right down to it, he doesn't believe that for a minute.

The difference is obvious. Bart is a white boy.

When Stephanie goes back to the castle, her mother will guard the door, belching flames, and Bart will never get through, which is sort of comforting. On the other hand, neither will I. If Stephanie goes to boarding school, her mother—who, of course, will have heard all about me from Dr. Grant, the great civil libertarian—will have left orders at the boarding school that no black male is to be allowed past the gate. They probably don't even need any such instructions. I hope she leaves the same orders for Bart. But what about all the other guys?

I bought some paper and a stamp at a grocery store and forced myself to write to Steffy. I used to give Stephanie suggestions when she was writing to Bart. I'd lie on the floor and dictate crazy sentences while she sat at her desk. "Don't go so fast!" she'd say, scribbling to keep up with me. But when I was the one with a blank sheet of paper in front of me, my mind was as blank as the paper.

"Dear Stephanie," I wrote, followed by a long pause while I thought of what to say next. Finally, "I heard a poem the other day that made me think of you, about a woman whose beauty 'burns in my heart a love-fire sharp like pain.' And then I learned this one, especially for you:

> I would liken you
> To a night without stars
> Were it not for your eyes.
> I would liken you
> To a sleep without dreams
> Were it not for your songs.

The poet is Langston Hughes, who was a friend of Grandmother Eugenia Brown, a long time ago." Pause again to feel guilty because I had actually memorized and recited that poem for Roxanne.

"I got your letter and I keep reading it over and over and feeling both good and bad when I read it—good that I have something from you, that you still love me, bad because everything seems to be falling apart. I believe if you think about it some more, you'll understand that I really had no choice except to leave, and not all of it had to do with Grant. Some of it had to do with me—finding out who I am, exactly.

"So here I am, almost two thirds of the way across the country, and I'm learning some things even if I don't know exactly what they are. That little sister of ours is one very smart kid. Yes, I spent a few days in Chicago, and someday I will tell you about that." But not all, not all.

"Tomorrow I expect to be at Grandma Sunderland's. By the time you get this, I'll probably be heading on to San Francisco. San Francisco is not my ultimate destination. My ultimate destination is to be with you, and somehow we will work it out, someday."

By the time I had written this much, I was so miserable and homesick for her, I thought I couldn't stand it. If it had been possible, I would have transported myself that second back to Pennsylvania, to Philadelphia or the Burg or wherever she was, and Stephanie and I would have taken off together somewhere. I would be the black knight rescuing the fair white maiden from the clutches of the evil king. I kind of liked that picture of myself.

But something else has been happening, I realize, and it's a totally unexpected discovery: I am enjoying the freedom of being on the road. I can see myself seizing Stephanie and running away with her, but at the same time I can see myself living the life of a vagabond, stopping for a week or a month or more in some funky little town on the prairie, and then moving on again. Nobody telling me what to do or when to do it or how to do it. It's possible there is some of my father in me after all, maybe more than a little of whatever it takes to split and not keep in touch with your family. Just keep rolling along, like Ol' Man River.

except their parents. I thanked the old geezer and started out. My plan was to find the place and look it over and then decide what I was going to do next.

It took me about three-quarters of an hour to find the big white mailbox with T. J. SUNDERLAND printed on it. The house is a long, low brick place with a green roof and a couple of big old trees growing close by, and it floats like a ship in an ocean of green. I was nervous, more nervous than I was in Chicago. I thought of driving back to town and calling, but I was already pretty far out of McClure, and if I went back to call and then turned around and came all the way out here again—well, I was tired. I decided to go up to the door and knock and see what would happen.

I drove down the long gravel road, churning up dust. A couple of kids were playing in the yard, and they stopped and stared at me as I got out of the car. I figured they were Tom Sunderland's kids, which would make them my cousins. Are they ever in for a surprise, I thought. "Hi," I said, "is your grandma at home?"

They kept staring. One of them, a boy about ten or so, stood up and wiped his hands on his jeans. "Who are you?"

"A friend of hers," I told the kid. "Would you go tell her she's got a visitor from Pennsylvania here to see her?"

The kid backed away toward the kitchen door, and when he got safely inside I could hear him screaming at the top of his lungs, "Ma! Ma! That guy looking for Grandma is out there!" The other kid, a girl about eight, never quit staring. I stared back.

"Hi," I said, squatting down, "what's your name?" But

the kid squirmed away from me, never taking her eyes off me. Nothing like Corky here, I thought.

Pretty soon the back door opened again, and a woman with her hair wound around pink plastic curlers stepped out into the yard. My mother may be fat, but I have never in my life seen her in plastic curlers.

"You looking for somebody?" the woman asked in a surly voice.

"I'm looking for Grace Sunderland," I said, but I knew this woman was not going to let a black dude near her mother-in-law without an explanation, and I had not figured out what it was going to be.

"She's laying down," the woman said. She had a flat, dull voice and flat, gray eyes, and she was looking me over very carefully. "What do you want with her?"

"It's personal," I said, but I knew that wouldn't cut it. Telling her the truth wouldn't either. I could feel her suspicion of me growing, like something cold and clammy. "There's something personal I have to talk to her about."

"I think you better leave and come back when my husband is here," she said, and then I saw her catch herself, knowing she should never have let on in the first place that he wasn't around. She tried to fix that. "I mean, when he's not busy. He's here," she lied quickly, "but he's too busy to come and talk to you now. And Granny isn't well at all."

"What's wrong with her?"

"Old age," she said, sticking out her pointy chin. "High blood pressure, glaucoma—that means she's going blind—

diabetes, arthritis, you name it. Ought to be in a home, if you ask me."

"Has she been sick a long time?" My best shot was to keep this woman talking.

"Long as I've been around, she has," the woman said, in a voice that made it clear she didn't like any of it. "Look, you mind telling me who you are?"

"My name is Dennis Brown."

You could see her face registering the inner workings of her brain as she struggled with a name that was familiar somehow, but she couldn't place it.

"And you know Grace Sunderland? You got the right person?"

"I got the right person, all right. Ma'am, please, won't you just let me see her for a few minutes? I'll only stay long enough to say hello, and then I'll go. I promise."

Her curiosity was getting her. She was figuring that if she let me into the house and hung around, she'd find out who I was and what I was doing there. Inside the house the phone started ringing, and she was pulled to answer it. I followed her toward the house, walking slow and easy so I wouldn't scare her. Actually I was scared, too, but not of her.

She backed into the kitchen and picked up the phone. "Hello." She listened for a few seconds. "He got here," she said and listened again. "I don't know. Call me back in ten minutes." She hung up. "Mr. Morris calling over from Milroy Center. Said you stopped there."

"Yes. He told me how to find your place."

She fiddled with one of the curlers, rewinding it and jabbing the pin back into it. "Granny's in here," she said.

I followed her down the hall to a small bedroom jammed with furniture. It smelled funny. Tom's wife said in a loud voice, "There's somebody here to see you, Granny," and stepped aside to make room for me. There was a shapeless mound under a faded green bedspread. Bright blue eyes stared up at me.

"Grandma, it's Dennis. I'm Lucy's son."

A hand reached up from the bedclothes and gripped my hand, surprisingly strong. "Dennis?" she repeated. "Lucy's boy? The colored boy?"

"Yes, Grandma."

"Well, well, well," she said, and squeezed my hand again. "Well, well, well."

I didn't know what else to say or do, so I stood there awkwardly with her hanging onto my hand. "I was on my way to California, and I thought I'd stop in and say hello." Which sounded pretty stupid to me, after I'd said it.

"Set down, Dennis," she said. "Loreen, is there a chair there for him?"

"Yes, Granny, there's a chair." The two kids had come into the house, and they were standing one by each of Loreen's elbows, looking at me as though I had just arrived from a distant planet.

"Set, Dennis, set," Grandma said. I sat on the old rocker next to her bed. "Closer," she said. "I don't see so good." I moved the rocker closer. "You hungry, son?"

"I can always eat," I said.

"Loreen, is there any of that pie left from yesterday?" she asked in a wheedling voice.

"I guess so." Loreen wouldn't win any prize for warm-hearted hospitality. She shuffled out, dragging the two kids, who kept staring back over their shoulders.

"I can't believe you're here, Dennis," she said.

"I can't either." Which was the truth.

"I don't see so good," she said again. "Tell me what you look like."

So I went through a description, tall and thin and so on. She reached out and touched my hair. She didn't ask, but I told her, "I've got dark skin, but it's not real dark. Like coffee with cream. A lot of cream."

"Uh-huh." I waited for her to ask me about my nose, but she didn't, and I don't know if it was because she forgot about wishing I could pass for Greek or if it didn't matter anymore. She hung onto my hand so tight my fingers were beginning to get numb.

"It's not good here, Dennis," she whispered. "I was all right on my own until I lost most of my sight. Tom insisted I come here, but Loreen don't like it at all."

Loreen came back with a piece of pie and a glass of orange drink, the two kids still tailing her. It was not a homemade pie—probably from the supermarket frozen food section. Loreen made no move to leave, just propped herself in the doorway and waited.

"Tell me about Lucy," Grandma said. "Is she all right? Grant? And little Corky?"

"They're all fine," I said. "Mother is still teaching French, and Grant is still taking care of people's hearts. Corky is terrific."

"I've never seen that child," she said. "Imagine, my own grandchild, and I've never seen her."

"How many are there of us?"

"You and Corky, and Bonnie and Billy." She went back to asking questions about Mother until finally Loreen got bored and shuffled off to the kitchen. The kids stuck around another few minutes, but then they got bored, too, and started punching each other. Loreen chased them outside. I ate the pie, genuine cardboard, and washed it down with the orange drink, which had been diluted to about half strength.

"How come you're in bed, Grandma?" I asked. "Are you sick?"

"Yes and no," she said. "I can't see, that is for sure. And some of it is I am getting old—seventy-six next October ninth. But somehow there don't seem to be any reason to get out of bed anymore. I started staying here more and more. It keeps me out of Loreen's hair."

"Her hair's already full of plastic curlers," I said.

Grandma laughed and covered her mouth with her hand. "I have to tell you," she said, "there are times when I'm glad I can't see so good no more. She always was a mess."

"She still is," I whispered. "How come you came here to live, then?"

"Because there was nowhere else to go. I couldn't keep the old place up anymore. Finally had to sell it, and it just about broke my heart. I hated coming here, but I couldn't see well enough to get around, and Tom had all that back trouble. Five operations and it's still not right. It seemed the best thing to do, but nobody wants an old woman living with them. No one wants to be the old woman, neither!"

"Do you get out at all? Do they take you places?"

She shook her head. "I haven't been outside these four walls for months and months."

"I'll take you out," I said.

She squeezed my hand again. "Mighty nice of you to offer, Dennis," she said. "Maybe tomorrow. Will you still be here tomorrow?"

"I guess that depends on Loreen, doesn't it? And she doesn't look too friendly. Maybe we better go today."

"Wait till Tom gets home. He's a good boy. He'll make sure you can stay. I can't invite you. It's not my home. You saw the trouble I had getting that pie for you. Did you eat it? Was it all right?"

"It was fine, Grandma."

"Pooh, it was not. That woman cannot cook to save her life. Everything from the freezer, if it's not out of a can. Sometimes I think she cooks that bad just to punish me."

"Doesn't Tom mind it?"

"He's a good boy, Tom, but he's a real Caspar Milquetoast."

"A what?"

"Oh, somebody from the funny papers years ago. 'The Timid Soul,' they called him. Couldn't be nicer, Tom

Sunderland, but not much backbone, especially when it comes to Loreen. And that little girl, Bonnie, is going to be just like her mother." Grandma had a habit of picking at the fuzz on the bedspread. It was developing bald patches. "But tell me more about Lucy. Oh, you don't know how I miss her!"

"Does she know you're here? Does she know you're sick, Grandma?"

"I wrote and told her I was moving here, sold the farm and all, but you know, there's lots you can't say in letters, and what good would it do, anyhow? She writes now and then. Told me you were graduating and all. In fact, she sent me a graduation picture last spring. I put it away. I didn't want to tell her I can't hardly see anymore."

"I didn't know about the picture." I wondered who else had gotten one. If Eugenia had one, I didn't know about it. "I didn't even know she was writing to you."

"Not often. Things happen in families, sad things. It hurts to think about it. We both said a lot years ago I think we regretted later, but you can't undo it, can't take back the words. Once they're said, they're said. We were both at fault."

She seemed not to remember the words were said because my mother married a black man. Or nigger, as I was pretty sure Loreen would say. I wanted to ask her about that, but I didn't know how to bring up the subject of my father. And then she did it herself, indirectly. "So you're going to California."

"Yes."

"It's a long way."

"Yes."

"Well, I'm real glad you stopped by to see us."

Suddenly the closeness was gone. She was acting like I was a stranger. But then I realized why. Loreen had come back, padding around like a clumsy cat in fluffy bedroom slippers. "Tom's here," she announced, and left.

"Now you'll meet your Uncle Tommy," Grandma said.

A tall man with a slight stoop ducked into the bedroom. He had thin, sandy hair and blue eyes like my mother's. He wore a light gray shirt with sweat stains under the arms and his name stitched in red above the pocket. "Hello, Mama," he said, and bent over and kissed her.

"Hello, son," she said, her voice sounding weaker than it had earlier. "How was your day?"

"As usual, as usual."

"Tommy, this here is your nephew Dennis, Lucy's boy, come all the way from Pennsylvania."

"Pleased to meet you," Tom said, looking me up and down with the cool blue eyes, and he stuck out his hand and I shook it. "Saw your Pennsylvania plates on the car outside," he said. "How goes the trip?"

"Oh, fine."

"Tommy, Dennis is going to be staying a few days, isn't that right, Dennis? I said I was sure you'd think it was all right to stay here."

"All right with me long's it's all right with Loreen."

"Oh, it's fine with her," Grandma said airily, but I wasn't so sure.

"Glad to have you here, Dennis," Tom said, and ducked out again.

Loreen turned out to be one of the truly awful cooks of this world. That was proved at suppertime, when we sat down at the kitchen table, all except Grandma, who got a tray in her room. I wondered if poor Tom and Grandma had to eat like this all the time, or if this was an especially bad example: a thin slab of ham cooked hard as bone and smothered in some kind of floury gravy, canned green beans, instant mashed potatoes, piles of white bread.

I had already attempted to attack the ham surgically, when Loreen's voice cut through the gravy. "That food ain't been blessed yet," she said. She still had the curlers in her hair; I wondered if she'd ever take them off. I put down my fork and stared at my lap while Tom intoned the blessing. The kids whined and complained all through dinner.

Bonnie's plate was loaded with nothing but bread and mashed potatoes drowning in a large lake of tan gravy. Dear little Bonnie, the clone of her mother, put down her spoon and glared at me. "You a nigger?" asked dear little Bonnie.

"Eat your supper, girl," snapped her mother.

"I *am*," said the tyke in a voice that just *asks* you to smack her. "I can eat and talk at the same time."

"Bonnie—" said Tom, but he quit there. What was it Grandma called him? Caspar Milquetoast.

"If you're a nigger, how come you're our cousin?" demanded Billy, her brother.

"My mother is your daddy's sister," I said, managing not to shove my plate of gravy in this kid's face.

"Then you can't be no nigger," said Bonnie—with Tom going "Bonnie . . . now, Bonnie"—"because we wouldn't 'low no niggers in our family. Isn't that right, Mama?"

Even Mama had the sense to look a little embarrassed. "She don't mean nothing by it," Loreen muttered.

"Isn't that *right*, Mama?" Bonnie persisted in a screech.

"Isn't a case of 'lowing or not," Loreen mumbled. "And now you just shut your mouth except to put food in it."

At this point Billy jumped in again. "Eeny meeny miney moe," he chanted, "catch a nigger by the toe. . . ."

"Will it stop all this bullshit if I say yes, I am a nigger?" I was about a half inch and a half second from total explosion.

"Mama, Mama, he used a bad word! Didn't he? He said bullshit, Mama. You always said we'd get our mouths washed out with soap if we said anything like that, especially at the dinner table!"

What a bunch. I said, "Bonnie, I know a whole lot of bad words. Bullshit is just for starters. They are so bad they will make your ears fall off and your nose turn blue. And if you call me a nigger again, I will say all of them, right at the dinner table." I shoved back my chair and walked out of the kitchen.

Grandma was sitting on the edge of her bed, struggling to spear some beans. "Next time I'll eat in here with you," I told her. She had spilled gravy all down the front of her. It looked pretty gross. "I'll clean you up. Just a second."

The Sunderlands' bathroom is decorated with little crocheted doodads. A yellow thing with purple flowers covers a can of spray used to disguise bathroom smells. A pink thing with a doll on top covers the spare roll of toilet paper. There is a crocheted cover decorated with butterflies on the toilet lid. I grabbed one of the soggy washcloths, wet it, and went back to clean off Grandma's front. She beamed at me. In her smile I saw my mother's smile.

"What do you think of Grant West?" she asked me.

"He's okay, I guess."

"I haven't seen much of Lucy since she married him. I hope this time she's happy."

"I think she is," I said, wondering if it was true.

"Makes you wonder what goes through people's heads when they get married."

"I don't think it has a whole lot to do with their heads," I said, and that made her laugh again. She covered her mouth so I wouldn't see she had taken out her false teeth. They were smiling on the bedside table.

"You're a smart young fellow, Dennis," she said. "You'll do all right."

"I hope so."

"What do you want to do, then? Are you going to college?"

Same old question, and I still didn't have the answer. "I don't know yet."

"Well, what do you like doing? Doesn't hurt to start there."

"I've been working with a furniture maker back in the Burg, and that's okay. But I don't think it's what I want to do for the rest of my life."

"I see. Tell me, do you have a girlfriend?"

Pause. Easy now. "Yes. At least I did when I left."

"And is she white or colored?"

"She's white."

"Do her parents approve?"

"No," I admitted.

"Wouldn't it be better to find one of your own kind?"

"If I knew what my kind was, maybe so. I mean, half of me is *your* kind." I probably shouldn't have opened that particular can of worms.

"Huh," she said.

We sat without talking. Dishes rattled in the kitchen. "How was your supper?" she asked.

"The food is pretty nasty," I said. "But the conversation was worse."

"What did they talk about?"

"The kids talked about niggers."

"Huh," she said again. "Shouldn't say this about my own grandkids, but they got awful bad mouths on 'em, both of them."

After a while Loreen came in. The plastic curlers were gone, and she was dressed up in a red skirt and a white blouse—both too tight—high heels, and several layers of makeup. "We're going now, Granny," she said, ignoring me. "You got everything you need?"

"If not, Dennis can get it for me," Grandma said.

"All right then." She left. Tom stuck his head in. He had on a clean shirt, and his limp hair was plastered against his pink scalp. "See you later," he said, nodding to us both. The kids ran after him. The pickup ground and caught and rumbled away.

"Church," Grandma said.

"Church?"

"Every Monday night there's a prayer meeting. I used to go too, when I was well."

I couldn't think of anything to say.

"Your mother take you to church and Sunday School?"

"No, ma'am."

"Don't know why I bothered to ask. She used to go all the time, till she went away to college. College changed her, and not for the better, if you ask me. Gave her all kinds of free-thinking ways."

Like marrying a black man, I thought, but I kept my mouth shut.

She didn't approve of my mother marrying my father because he was black. What did she think of her son marrying that stupid, ugly, mean woman just because she's white? I guess people don't think of things like that generally. I do.

Then she got the idea that I should read the Bible to her.

"It would mean a lot," she said. I had no interest in any of that stuff, although I didn't want to tell her that. It doesn't make sense to me, and if it doesn't make sense, then what's the point?

"I used to read Scriptures every day, before my sight

began to fail," Grandma said. Her life was divided into several parts—before and after Roy died, before and after her sight began to fail, before and after the move to Uncle Tom's house. You would think that Loreen, or especially Tom, might take some time—say, once a week or so—to read to her. Or maybe just a few minutes a day.

The Bible has been hers since she was a little girl and has her name stamped in gold on the worn leather cover, Grace Agnes Helfrecht. She thought the Book of Exodus was what she wanted. It looked like a long book, with a whole lot of chapters, but she said if I just took a few at a time, it would go quick, and there was a lot we could skip over.

"On second thought," she said, "start with Genesis. There are some real good stories in Genesis. It isn't going to mean much to you if you don't begin at the beginning and get the whole picture."

"In the beginning," I began, and I thought, how can people really believe all this stuff? But we went through it chapter by chapter, verse by verse. I expected to be bored out of my mind, but actually they are pretty good stories.

First there was the Creation, and then Adam and Eve, the serpent and the forbidden fruit, which got them thrown out of the Garden of Eden. They had two sons, Cain and Abel, and one killed the other one and had to spend the rest of his life wandering around. Next came the story of Noah's ark. God was extremely annoyed and punished everybody except Noah and his family by sending a flood. But Noah built an ark and took pairs of every animal on board and they floated around while it rained for forty days and forty nights. I liked that story. There was a rainbow at the end. All stories ought to end with rainbows. I always thought we had a complicated family with a lot of crazy problems, but that was before Grandma got me reading the Bible to her. Those people were *really* screwed up, and it seemed to me God was always making matters worse. Grandma says this is because I don't understand it. But I think I understand it well enough.

Tape 9

Tuesday, July 15th, in Nebraska.

I set my tent up outside, under the tree. It seems easier than putting Loreen to any trouble, which would make things worse. They left the door unlocked so I can use the bathroom. What I wanted was a shower, which I got, even with all the crap she has hanging around in there, her underwear draping the shower rod and so on. P.S., the woman's underwear is as ugly as she is, and what would you expect?

Bonnie and Billy wanted to come in the tent with me. They had never been in a tent before. Bonnie still looks at me as though I belong in a cage with the other gorillas.

The only reason I'm staying here is to get to know Grandma. All I've known about her is what my mother told me, mostly stories of how she and Grandpa reacted when Mother married my dad.

I understand the bad feeling between my mother and _her_ mother, but I thought they got over it. Nebraska is a long way from Pennsylvania, but you'd think Mother would have come out to visit. She said that when Corky was old enough, they'd go together the way she and I did it, although I couldn't picture Corky and Mother on a bus for several days. Grant is too busy for family visits, he says. When he can take some time off, they go to a cabin by a lake in Vermont, which has belonged to his family for generations. He says when he goes away it's to relax, not to deal with families. Mother has tried to get him to take a trip somewhere, to go to Europe. She's still talking about Paris.

All Grant wants to do is sit in his cabin at the lake, dressed up in his L.L. Bean camp outfit. Sometimes he takes the boat out and drops a fishing line over the side and never catches a thing. It's a pretty place, and Mother was very excited the first couple of times we went up there. But then she got bored with it, not being much of an outdoors person, and she began to talk about going to Boston or San Francisco for a week.

"I need to relax, Lucy," Grant would say. "You've got to understand that I'm under tremendous pressure."

"Grant, why on earth can't you relax in Boston or Paris just as well? I'm under pressure, too, remember, and I need a change!"

They go on like this all the time, but Grant always wins.

In a way I can see why Mother didn't want to make the trip out here, even though Grandma would have liked to see her. Grandmother Eugenia said the reason the Brown side of the family was against the marriage was because the Sunderlands were not their social equals. That seemed snobby, but when I watch these scruffy, bigoted kids with no manners at all and listen to Loreen screeching at them, I think, Eugenia, you've got a point.

But she was wrong about Grace Sunderland. Grandma may not speak perfect English, and she may not know about classical music and poetry and art and all the things that Eugenia Brown does, but she's got a good heart. And a good heart is worth a whole lot.

Last night in my tent outside Tom Sunderland's house, I settled down with a flashlight and Eugenia's copy of *Othello, the Moor of Venice*, by William Shakespeare. We had studied *Romeo and Juliet* in high school, so I knew this was going to be a struggle. Shakespeare was an Englishman, but the English he wrote three hundred and fifty some years ago doesn't seem to have much to do with the English we speak. Our class went through the play line by line, translating all the strange words that don't mean the same thing now that they did back then or don't even exist anymore, by which time I didn't give a flip about the Montagues and the Capulets. I was glad Eugenia had told me the plot of *Othello*.

Reading the play gave me a whole lot to think about. Honesty, for one thing, and jealousy, for another. The green-eyed monster, Iago calls it. The only thing Othello the Moor had to complain of about Desdemona, who was obviously crazy about him, was what Iago planted in his mind. He became convinced that she was sleeping with Cassio, and that drove him completely berserk. I remember how jealous I was of Bart Schwartz, Stephanie's boyfriend before she came to live with us. But later, I thought it was good cover for us, so she kept on writing to him after she and I fell in love. She was deceiving Grant just the same way Desdemona was deceiving her father. And Brabantio, the father, warns Othello, before Iago has even started his dirty little game: "She has deceived her father, and may thee."

Once you start thinking about it, jealousy can drive you right out of your mind. Now that I know Steffy is going back to Philadelphia soon, I can guess that she's going to be seeing Bart in spite of her mother and probably falling for him all over again. And what can I do about it? Nothing. I'm here, she's there, and who knows when I'll ever see her again.

Jealousy isn't something that worries me while she's in the Burg. I know there isn't anybody around there she'd be interested in. I know she's reminded of me all the time. She's okay there, and I have no reason to get jealous. Philadelphia will be different. I have never seen Bart Schwartz, and for all I know, he is Mister Wonderful. I don't need any friend like Iago to put poison in my ear. All I'll need is a word from Stephanie that she's seen him, and I'll probably go berserk, too.

There is another side to this: the Roxanne side. I was not being loyal to Stephanie when I was hanging out with Roxanne. I wasn't even *thinking* of Steffy most of the time in Chicago. All I could think of was Roxanne, who is sexy, sexy, sexy, the kind of woman you brag about to your friends. I wouldn't do that with Stephanie.

At the time I thought it didn't make any difference, or at least not much, because Stephanie is a long way off, and what I was doing with Roxanne had nothing to do with Stephanie. If she didn't know about it, how could it hurt her? Othello had a few words to say about that. "He that is robbed, not wanting what is stol'n, Let him not know't, and he's not robbed at all." When he didn't know about Cassio, he didn't think about it and it didn't bother him. So if Stephanie didn't know about Roxanne, she wouldn't be hurt. And I won't be hurt if I don't know about Bart.

On the one hand, I'm almost eighteen years old, and Steffy will be seventeen in a couple of months. We're thousands of miles apart—which might as well be millions —and naturally she's going to be seeing other guys after Grant calms down, and I'm going to be with other girls, and who knows if we can ever get it together and keep it together?

On the other hand, Steffy is not just anyone, and I am not just anyone. We have a bond, partly because of who our parents are, and partly because of who we are. We are part of the same family, even if Mother and Grant decide to split, which could happen, given the statistics of marriage and divorce. There is always Corky to keep us glued to-gether. Corky is our sister, and with somebody like Corky for a sister, we're bound to keep in touch.

This morning Uncle Tom called me in for breakfast. He does only a little farming and works in town full-time for a contruction company. "Used to be strong as an ox," he said, digging into a huge breakfast, "but that was before my back trouble. Used to work construction, made some good money with that, but now all I can do is keep the books, and it's not hardly worth the trouble. Still, it puts food on the table."

He was on his way to his job in town, and Loreen was going with him to do some shopping. She made a big point of that: "We got an extra mouth to feed, so I have to get some food in here." She grabbed Bonnie and Billy to take them along, although they plainly wanted to stay home and observe me. "He wants to talk to Granny," she said.

"I'm going to get my hair done while I'm in town," Loreen announced. "Might as well take advantage of having somebody here to look after her, take her to the bathroom and all. It won't be long till she won't even want to do that, and you can guess what *that* is going to mean for me. You don't know how much having her here has tied me down, her being not quite all there, know what I mean?" She tapped her skull. "Now, don't let her talk you into anything. She's a real manipulator, know what I mean?"

"That's okay," I said. "I don't mind staying with her. We get along fine."

Off they went in the pickup truck. "Not quite all there," Loreen said. Meaning what? A little crazy? Who *wouldn't* be crazy, living with Loreen and her brood. I know a kid whose grandmother has Alzheimer's disease, in which your memory just goes. I never knew not being able to remember something could make life so miserable, but it sure did for that family. I don't think that's what's wrong with Grandma. I think what's mainly wrong is that she's lonely.

Soon as the family was out the door, I went to her room. "Good morning, Dennis," she said. "You sleep all right?"

"Yeah, fine." Which was only partly true—*Othello* kept me awake for a long time. "How're you feeling today?"

"Well, maybe a little better. I don't know. Funny thing, I was all ready to say I don't feel so good, which is what I say every day, and then I thought, Dennis doesn't want to hear that. So I'm going to say I'm feeling a little better."

Her voice did sound stronger. "Let's go somewhere," I said.

"Where?"

"I don't know. Someplace you'd like to go. If you don't mind riding in my old heap."

Slowly she pushed herself up. Slowly her feet and legs came out from under the covers. They were old lady's legs, milky white with bulging blue veins. Cautiously she felt around for a beat-up pair of men's brown slippers and worked her feet into them. "Give me a hand here, will you, Dennis? We're going to the bathroom."

I didn't much care for this idea, but I helped her off the bed and draped her robe around her and steered her out the door and down the hall. "Now you'll have to help me *set*," she said, "but that's all."

I have never done anything like this in my life, and I was real nervous about it. I steered her to the toilet, thinking, Oh boy, oh boy, but she sat down on it like a hen on a nest. "Now I'm fine," she said, and waved me away. I got out of there quick. When I heard the toilet flush she called me, and I went back to lever her up and get her back to her room. Only then she didn't need quite so much help, and she steered herself more or less straight down the hall. She plopped down on the edge of the bed, but she didn't lie down.

"I think we can do this," she said. "I'll tell you where things are, and you find them, and I'll get dressed and we'll go."

She directed me to various drawers and the closet, and eventually I got things together for her. She had me bring her a pan of warm water and soap and a washcloth and towel, and I left her with everything lined up around her on the bed. While she got washed, I looked the place over.

It felt poor, as though nobody cared or had the time or energy to care. The kitchen was a mess; Loreen and the kids had left all the sticky breakfast dishes. I decided the least I could do was clean this all up. I cleared the table and washed the dishes and stacked them on the counter, which didn't look very clean either, but I was not going to do Loreen's housecleaning for her. The worst moment came when I put the milk away. The refrigerator was a very bad scene—botulism and salmonella growing like crazy among the old food. Probably a good idea for me to cook my own meals outside on my Coleman stove and save everybody a lot of grief.

"Dennis!" Grandma called. She was still sitting on the edge of her bed, but she was dressed up in a dark blue dress with white polka dots. "How do I look?"

"You look nice," I said, "except for your hair. Do you have a brush somewhere?" Her white hair was tangled and matted. There wasn't much I could do with it, even when I found a brush. "Maybe you could wear a hat," I suggested. But we couldn't find one, and so I got a scarf to tie around her hair, and her big black purse from another drawer, and we were ready to go.

I helped her out to my car, shoving and hauling her onto the front seat, which I had cleared off. "Now where shall we go?"

"Just *go*, Dennis. I don't much care where to."

I drove down the long dusty lane to the country road and turned the opposite of the way I had come in. Grandma knew the road by heart, knew each farm's owner and history. "When you come to a crossroads down a ways, just past a row of mailboxes, turn right," she said.

I did. "Now what?"

"I'll tell you," she said.

Grandma was humming a little tune under her breath. I followed the flat ribbon of road between rows of green fields with farmhouses set far back at the ends of dusty lanes.

"Next left," she said. "Be on the lookout for a lane between two big spruce trees. Stop when you get there."

I found the trees and pulled the car over next to them. At the end of the rutted lane was a white house, plain as a shoebox but surrounded by flowers. Red roses climbed over a white trellis by the door, yellow ones bloomed around a birdbath, and pink and white ones lined the lane.

"That's it," she said. "That's my old home. How are my roses?"

"They're beautiful. There must be a million of them."

"I had the prettiest rose gardens you've ever seen in your life," she said. "You can't see it from the road, but out in back there's an arbor that runs from one end of the yard to the other, covered with a rambler like the one by the front door. Used to start blooming in June and go all summer. The ones along the lane are the prize specimens. I won some blue ribbons with them at the state fair." She smiled to herself. "How do they look, Dennis? Are the new people taking care of them?"

"Yes," I said, thinking of Loreen's front yard, which is nothing but bare dirt and some dry grass and not a single flower. "The roses are doing fine."

"The yellow ones, I think they're to the left. Those were the ones I put in right before I decided to move in with Tom and Loreen. That was hard, Dennis, I can tell you. I lived all my married life in that house. That's where your grandfather and I went to live when he came back from the army at the end of World War II. Your mother was a little bit of a thing, maybe three, and Tommy was only just about born. Too bad you never got to know your grandfather. He was a fine-looking feller! Lot younger than me. Guess you knew that."

"No, I didn't know that." I took another look at the house with the roses and started up Mary again.

"Yep, ten years younger. He was just a kid when I met

him, not a whole lot older than you, and I was already an old maid of thirty. But we liked each other fine. Not sure we would of got married if he hadn't been going off to war, but he joined up right after Pearl Harbor, and when he came home on his first leave, he said, 'Well, come *on*, Gracie,' and I grabbed my hat and gloves and we did it. Then off he went to North Africa, and your mother come along the next Christmas, and your Uncle Tom after the war was over. And that house is where we moved, so your granddaddy could get back to farming again."

Flash—my mind went back to Roxanne, six years older than me. I wonder if Grandma taught Grandpa anything, and then I got embarrassed for even thinking about such things. But I decided to ask her something anyway: "Did it make any difference to you and Grandpa that you were ten years older?"

"Not one bit," she said. "Seems to me that's the way it *ought* to be, 'stead of the other way around. But it still left me a widow at sixty-four. He was only fifty-four when he passed away."

That made me kind of sorry I asked the question. "Where to now, Grandma?"

"There's a white church up near the crossroads," she said. "Would you please stop there?"

It was a small church with a steeple and a cemetery next to it and a low white picket fence. "Here we are," I said.

"I never missed a Sunday. In fact I was honored for perfect attendance," she said. "And your mother was, too.

She used to sing in the junior choir and go to youth fellow-ship every Sunday night. Tom was pretty regular, too, but not like Lucy. Does she go to church in Vicksburg?"

"No, ma'am."

"And do you go, Dennis?"

"No, ma'am. I don't know anything about it."

"Well, of *course* you don't know anything about it if you don't go," she snorted. "How in the world would you learn?"

"Mother said it was my choice. It was up to me if I wanted to go or not. But I said I wasn't particularly in-terested."

She climbed out and we moved slowly up the path toward a pair of red doors. "Pardon me for saying so, Dennis, but for all her education and degrees, your mother is plain stupid. I don't like to criticize her, because she seems to have done a good job raising you. You're a nice boy. But it is plain stupid to expect a child to make a choice on a subject on which there is no information. Now if she had seen to it that you went every Sunday, got your Bible instruction, went through confirmation, took you and stayed there with you at worship every Sunday, and then at the right age, maybe eighteen, she gave you a choice and you said no, then I'd say she had done right."

I got a little raked about that. Mother and I argue about things, but generally we get along fine. Probably better than most guys I know get along with their parents. Grant is the only real problem, and the only time I get really upset with her is when Grant comes down on me for something and she takes his side. So I didn't like it at all that Grandma had those things to say, criticizing her. It wasn't anybody's business but Mother's if she sent me to church or not, and it wasn't anybody's business but mine if I wanted to go or not.

The red doors were locked, so we walked around to the side. An old man was working in the yard, pulling up weeds. "Is this Mr. Clay?" Grandma sang out.

"Yes, Mrs. Sunderland, it surely is." He straightened up slowly. "And how does it go for you today? I haven't seen you here for months and months."

"Well, I haven't been out for quite a while. But I'm having a visit from my grandson Dennis. Lucy's boy. You remember Lucy?"

"Well, well, well, so this is Lucy's boy." The old man stepped closer for a better look. You could see things go click in his head and then register clearly on his lined face. It was disturbing to be able to read his thoughts so clearly. I wondered what Grandma and Grandpa told their friends and neighbors and the people in the church when Mother made her rash move. And I wondered if Grandma had forgotten that I was a dirty little secret, or if she didn't care anymore.

I decided she didn't care.

I guided her over the rough ground and through a little gate in the fence to the cemetery. The next stop was a low, gray granite tombstone with SUNDERLAND carved in it. Under that it said *Roy D. 1920–1974*. Next to it was *Grace H. 1910–19——*. There was a blank space, and I realized the space was left for the date she would die, just as a space was left in the ground for her, next to Roy D. "They haven't carved the second date in on mine yet, have they?" she asked, and for a second I didn't know it was her joke.

"Just the '19.' The rest is blank."

"Shows you what pessimists they all are. I was thinking I might hang around till the year 2000, just to show them. They've had me with one foot in the grave for years. That would fix Loreen, wouldn't it? If I lived another fourteen years?"

"It's not impossible. You could do it. You'd only be ninety." And I will be thirty-two when the year 2000 comes in. What a New Year's Eve bash that will be.

"I'm thinking of doing it just to spite her. But the thought of living with that woman for another fourteen years is almost more than I can bear."

"Isn't there some way you can get rid of her?"

"Well, Dennis, she is Tom's wife and that is their home. I can't very well throw her out, now can I? I will confess to you that I sometimes hope she'll meet somebody, the butcher at the supermarket, the man who comes to fix the washing machine, *anybody*, and just run off with him. Sometimes I lie in bed at night and pray that she will leave. Isn't that awful, Dennis? It's probably a very bad sin, and I commit it almost every night."

"I don't think it's a really terrible sin." I remember how I used to lie in bed and wish that Grant would split, split, split.

"It would take a lot of prayer and probably a minor miracle to get her out of there. I tell you, only my good-hearted son Tom would put up with some of her tricks for more than five minutes. Besides that, she's a miserable housekeeper."

"Yeah, she is pretty bad. I'm surprised the whole family hasn't dropped over from food poisoning."

Mr. Clay had unlocked the side door of the church, and we navigated in that direction to get out of the hot sun. Grandma sat down with a sigh on a wooden pew. It was dim and cool and peaceful there. A big Bible lay open on a stand up front, and a plain wooden cross stood on the altar beneath a stained-glass window with a picture of a shepherd and a flock of sheep. The shepherd wore a halo around his head and carried a lamb in one arm. Off to one side of the church was a little electric organ.

"Do you have to stay there? Couldn't you go somewhere else?"

"An old folks' home, most likely. That's what Loreen wants me to do. They gave me one of the bedrooms, but that means Bonnie and Billy have to share, and they're growing up and can't do that for much longer. I know it drives Loreen crazy that I'm still alive and taking up all that space, when Bonnie and Billy are at an age that they need separate rooms. When it gets to the point that you're a burden, it's probably better if you just go shoot yourself and get it over with."

"Grandma . . ."

She reached over and patted my hand. "Oh, Dennis,

don't worry! I'm not going to do anything silly. But it has crossed my mind."

I sat there building up a good case of loathing against Loreen, and some against Tom, too, for letting her be so mean. "Does Tom know how she treats you?"

"She treats him the same way. I hate to admit it, but Tom is a weak man. At first I was glad when he married a strong woman like Loreen, because I figured she'd pull him through. I hadn't figured on her getting so sour as she got older. She was a real pretty girl once upon a time, if you can believe that."

"I can't."

"What does your mother look like now, Dennis? I haven't seen her in such a long time, I don't even know how to picture her."

"To tell you the truth, she's overweight. I mean, she's *fat*, that's all. But she's still pretty. And she hasn't gotten sour at all. Sometimes you want to smack her, she's so cheerful."

That made Grandma smile. "Yes, she always was the sunshine in the family. But a little bit of a rebel, too. I was always afraid she'd end up in trouble."

"I guess you think she did. Marrying my dad."

"Huh. Well, you're right. I'm not going to deny it. I was just sick to my stomach when I found out what she had done. And her father was fit to be tied! But I've been on this earth long enough to learn that eventually things work out somehow. God sees to that. I had a hard time seeing that God would make me change my feelings about James

Brown. Nothing against the man, but I thought he should have had more sense if she didn't. He's colored, he knows what it's like, and if he really loved her he wouldn't have thought only of himself but of her and of what it would do to her life. What she would have to put up with."

"Put up with people like Loreen and Bonnie, for instance."

"Well, you have to understand that Loreen goes to a church that preaches that some people are saved and some aren't, and some people are better than others in the sight of God. She has been saved. Her big mission in life is to bring me to the Lord. I keep telling her I don't *need* to be saved, that my soul is just fine, thank you very much, and I already *am* with the Lord. But it has to be her way, you see. And Bonnie is just like her. Billy, bless his heart, takes after his dad, just as good as gold, and he don't stand a chance against them two women."

I don't think Billy is as good as gold, but I was not going to argue that point. I had seen Billy helping himself to some food out of my pack, canned sardines that I had stashed as emergency rations, but that might be because he was starving to death on his mother's cooking.

"Dennis, why don't you play something on that organ?"

"I don't know how to play an organ."

"Pooh. It's just a simple little electric thing. Go fool around with it and see what happens."

"Are you sure that would be all right?"

"I'm sure. Go ahead."

I pushed the ON switch and felt the organ hum to life.

Then I tried a couple of chords. Funny, not at all like a piano, but a lot like my electronic keyboard. I pushed down some of the levers across the top and found that I could make the thing sound completely different with each combination. After about five minutes of my experimentation, Grandma lost patience.

"Never mind all that, Dennis. Do you know this?" She began to sing in her quavery old-lady voice, "Amazing Grace, how sweet the sound, that saved a wretch like me. . . ." I followed along, picking out the melody, adding chords. "I once was lost but now I'm found, was blind but now I see."

Somehow it sounded right. Imagine, Dennis James Brown, playing in church. I looked up at Grandma, who was both the choir and the congregation, and the tears were running down her cheeks.

"Oh, Dennis, that is the most beautiful thing," she said, and began fishing around in her black handbag for a handkerchief. "I could just set here all day and listen to you play."

I'm a sucker for an audience. I wished I knew a couple more hymns to play for her, because it made her feel good. Then I shut down the organ and we went back to my car. She was smiling and smiling. Hard to believe this is the same sad-looking soul I saw lying helpless in bed yesterday.

"What now, Grandma?"

"Take me back to the house. I want to get there before Loreen comes back and find some things to show you."

Tape 10

Still Tuesday, July 15th, still the Sunderlands' in McClure, Nebraska, and I'm telling about yesterday with Grandma.

We crept around like a pair of burglars. Grandma wanted to find some old family albums, but there was no telling where they might have been buried in Loreen's messy house.

"The first thing she did when I moved in here was to pack away my things I'd had for years. 'You can't see nothing anyway, Granny,' she said. 'What do you want this stuff all around for?' Baby pictures of your mother and Tom, and my wedding picture with Roy. I want to find out what she did with them."

If I knew anything about Loreen, I would bet those pictures were long gone, thrown out with the trash; on the other hand she's too messy to bother throwing them out. She seems to have a hard time parting with old newspapers, for instance, which are stacked around the kitchen and family room in collapsing piles.

"Where should we start? Attic or basement? And how about the garage?"

"I can't do the stairs, Dennis," she said. "I'm about all played out as it is." She sat down heavily on a kitchen chair and fanned herself, trying to catch her breath. All of a sudden I got scared. Grandma was sick, and maybe she was going to get a lot sicker. Maybe she was going to have a heart attack, and it would be my fault. Or Loreen would say it was, and maybe she'd be right.

"I think you ought to go lie down," I said.

"No! I'm fine. Just not used to this, is all. They treat me like I'm an invalid, and I act like one, and it's my own fault, not standing up to her. But I don't want warfare in the house, I couldn't tolerate that. It would kill me. So I give in, every time."

"Maybe I should fix you something to eat," I suggested, looking around at the disaster area called a kitchen. "Are you hungry?" I remembered that I had some food in the car. "I'll fix us a picnic," I said. "If you have nothing against sardines."

We went outside under the big tree, and I took a can of sardines from my pack—one Billy hadn't found—and made a couple of sandwiches. "Just wonderful, Denny," she said. "Been a long time since anything tasted this good." I would have enjoyed it more if my tooth hadn't been hurting again. After we ate, I took a look around the garage and the shed next to it. There were stacks and stacks of boxes. I opened a couple: old magazines, rusty kitchen stuff, old clothes. When I was ready to give up, I opened one more box, and there they were, the pictures Grandma had been talking about. Under it was a box of scrapbooks and framed photographs. I lugged it all out to the picnic table.

There is a story that goes with each item, and by the time we had worked our way through most of it, I knew a whole lot about the Sunderland family.

Inside one of the cartons was a shoebox of Grandpa Roy's World War II army stuff. "He believed it was his patriotic duty," she said. "His father was in poor health, couldn't run the farm no more. So Roy and his brother Clayton ran it. Clayton was married and had two kids, and Roy wasn't married yet. He would of been drafted anyway. So he turned the farm over to Clayton and went up to Ogallala and enlisted in January of 1942. He was gone for about six weeks in basic training, then he come home on leave, we got married, and they shipped him overseas. I moved out to the farm with Clayton and Pearl while Roy was running around North Africa and Italy. We worked night and day to keep the farm going. I didn't find out I was carrying your mother until he was overseas."

She showed me a picture of a smiling soldier. He came home to find a little blond, blue-eyed girl who was a total stranger. There was a picture of him, still in his uniform, holding her, and she was crying. Among stacks of old black and white snapshots, curling in on themselves and nested together, was a framed picture of my mother in a cap and gown, graduating from the University of Nebraska, Class of 1964. She was a celebrity in the family, the only one who went to college. Yellowed newspaper clippings were neatly pasted in a scrapbook with her name on the front: *Lucy Sunderland Named Yearbook Editor. Lucy Sunderland 1st in Class. Lucy Sunderland Wins Scholarship. Lucy Sunderland Wins French Prize. Lucy Sunderland to Study in Paris.*

"Your mother was so *bright*," Grandma said. I had never thought of her being either bright or not bright, but that made me feel proud. "And a hard worker. She was first in her high school class, and she won the prize for French literature in her senior year in college. The only thing I can say against her is that she's never been very practical. Head always in the clouds. That drove her daddy crazy, although God knows she was the apple of his eye."

"Until she married my father." I couldn't resist it. Couldn't keep my mouth shut.

Grandma sighed. "That's true. He refused to accept that. It went completely against his grain. He felt that it was a sin, a break with the natural order. And to tell you the truth, Dennis, I had to agree with him. But still, I kept saying, 'She's our *daughter*, Roy, our own flesh and blood.' And he'd say, 'I know that, but wrong is wrong.' "

"I guess I don't understand what's so wrong about it. Just because a person's skin color is different."

"I don't know as I can explain it in any way that will make sense to you, Dennis, but it's more than just the color of the skin. A Negro, a colored person, is different inside as well as out."

"How?"

"God made them different, that's all I can tell you, and it's a sin when different kinds come together. For instance, there is scientific proof that black people are not as intelligent as white people. They're smarter than animals, but not as smart as white people. That is why they are always on the bottom of society."

"What about me?" I was shaking, and I could hear my voice trembling. "That makes me different, too, doesn't it? Because there's every bit as much of him in me as there is of her. I'm just as much a black person as I am a white person."

"Well, you see, Dennis, there you have it. And you'll never fit in either place, and that's the tragedy of it."

It didn't feel like tragedy to me, but it felt sad. I was sad that my grandmother, who is a nice, kind lady, has such strange ideas about black people. I'll bet she never knew any. How would she know if they were "different" from white people? What would she make of Eugenia, and a whole family of smart blacks who had been to college? I guess I knew it wouldn't make any difference; her mind was made up. But I tried it anyway:

"You should meet my other grandmother, Eugenia Brown. She's a college graduate; everybody in the family is. And they're all intelligent people with good jobs." I remembered the voice of Paul Robeson and the poetry of Langston Hughes, but I knew this wasn't any kind of rational debate in which one side can prove something to the other side. It was the way Grandma felt, and no amount of *proving* was going to change that.

"Well, there is always *some* folks who try real hard and rise above their nature. But that doesn't change their nature, or what they came from."

Believe it or not, after this conversation I was actually glad to see Loreen and Bonnie and Billy come bouncing up the lane in their pickup. Loreen had been to the beauty parlor, and her hair was now the color of hay, stacked on top of her head like a haymow and varnished to keep it in place. You could see that she believed she looked beautiful. Grandma told me Loreen was a cheerleader in high school and prom queen in her senior year. It's hard to see much of that left, and I don't think Bonnie holds much promise. Both Bonnie and Billy had been clipped like small dogs and had white lines around their faces that had been covered with hair while the rest got suntanned.

"Don't suppose you'd want to help unload all these groceries," Loreen said, starting to tug a brown paper sack out of the bed of the pickup. I left Grandma thumbing through the scrapbooks. We set the sacks down on the table, and Loreen started putting things away while I brought in the rest of the sacks. I wondered if Loreen would notice the change in the kitchen. "You'd better get her back to bed," she said. "She gets real ornery when she gets tired from being out so long."

I went outside again. "You ready to go lie down?"

"Loreen's idea, I suppose," Grandma said with a sigh. "Yes, Dennis, I guess I am. No sense making trouble."

I felt like a jailer leading a prisoner back to her cell. "Let's figure out someplace to hide the scrapbooks and pictures so she don't find them," Grandma whispered. "Next time she'll probably just burn them, since she's not in any of them."

"I'll put them back in the shed," I whispered back. "Then we'll think of a better place."

But in the meantime Bonnie and Billy had found them and were spreading them all over the table. A gust of wind had lifted some off the table and sent them spinning over the dry grass toward the field. "I'm putting them away now," I said. "Billy, why don't you go catch the ones that are blowing away?"

"They're no good anyway," Billy said, not moving.

"Why do you think they're no good?"

"Just dumb pictures," Bonnie said.

"They're not dumb. And they're Grandma's. We're going to put them away for her."

"You put them away, then," she said, and the two kids slid off the picnic bench and ran off.

My cousins—blood relatives. Oh boy. I rounded up all the old snapshots and packed them away again.

Loreen announced we were going to have a special dinner, Uncle Tom's favorite. Not just everyday greasy pork chops and canned beans. "This is real good," she said. "This is what I make for church suppers."

Tuna noodle casserole with cream of mushroom soup is one of the really awful inventions. I like tuna fish, and I like noodles, I even like mushrooms, but somehow when you put them all together with that canned stuff that tastes like wallpaper paste, it's horrible. What made this a company dish, Bonnie explained, when the casserole arrived on the table, was the mashed cornflakes sprinkled on top. In fact, that was the only part she and Billy liked. They scraped off the crust that had formed and left the pale, gluey mush for the rest of us. We also had canned peas and ice cream and Oreo cookies. Bonnie and Billy licked off the icing and left the cookies, several pairs of them, watching TV the whole time.

The television is on from the time they roll out of bed in the morning until they fall asleep at night. It goes through meals. It's like a member of the family. I thought about getting them to watch Bill Cosby. Forget telling them about Paul Robeson and Marian Anderson; why not let them look at some good TV shows and see that blacks are just like everybody else.

"You ever watch 'The Bill Cosby Show'?" I asked, chasing around my peas.

"Yeah."

"Sometimes."

"Pretty good show, don't you think?"

"It's okay."

"I'd ruther watch 'Magnum.' It's more better. And 'Miami Vice.' "

"The reason I mention it is because Bill Cosby shows black people with good jobs. Professionals. She's a lawyer and he's a doctor, right?"

"Aw, you don't believe that stuff, do you? It's TV. It's not real life."

"But some black people do get to be doctors and lawyers, Billy."

He looked at me as though I wasn't very bright. "Not here, they don't."

"Niggers are dumb," Bonnie said, screwing open another Oreo.

"Says who?"

Her shoulders made a big shrug. "Don't nobody have to say it, 'cause everybody knows it."

"How do you know it unless somebody says it?"

"Well, just look at *you*. Asking a lot of dumb questions."

"That'll be enough of that," Uncle Tom said in a mild, slow voice. And I gave up completely on his favorite dinner.

I went in to talk to Grandma. She wanted me to read the Bible to her again.

This time the story was about Moses leading the Israelites out of slavery in Egypt to the promised land. In my mind I could hear Paul Robeson singing, "Let my people go." Something clicked and I knew what that song was about: before the Civil War, black people in America had been in slavery and needed someone like Moses to lead them out. But after the Israelites got out of Egypt, they had to wander around in the desert for forty years. Even with God taking care of them, it was no easy thing.

* * *

Saturday, July 19th. New problem. The tooth that had been giving me a little jolt of pain every time something cold hit it suddenly exploded into total misery a couple of days ago. I've been telling myself that whatever is wrong with the tooth would hold off until I got to San Francisco, but that was obviously impossible. It's the first toothache I've ever had, and I hope it's the last. I searched through the medicine cabinet in Loreen's bathroom, but the best I could come up with was aspirin. I took a couple, but they didn't even touch it.

All I could think about was the pain.

I finally told Grandma about it, and she announced that she was taking me to the dentist. *She* was taking *me*. Her dentures were bothering her, she said, and we might just as well go together.

So yesterday Grandma put on her polka-dot dress, the one she wore to go to the church the day I played the organ for her, and I gulped down a couple more aspirin and drove her into Milroy Center. The receptionist took Grandma in first, while I flipped through old *Time* magazines, months out of date. Pretty soon Grandma came out, feeling her way along the wall. Then it was my turn.

The dentist, Dr. Decker, took an X ray and gave me the bad news: I need a root canal and a crown. When I asked what it would cost, his estimate was about three times what I have left to get me to San Francisco. And I didn't want to borrow any money from Grandma.

"Isn't there anything else you can do?" I asked him.

"I can clean it up and give you a temporary filling and some medication for the infection. You've got an abscess. But sooner or later—probably sooner—you're going to have to take care of it right."

He gave me a shot that numbed out my whole jaw and went to work on the tooth. "Your grandmother is a different person than the last time she was here," he said, grinding away at what was left of my tooth. "I thought at first she was on some new medication, but she says nothing's changed. I think she's awfully glad you're here to visit. Too bad you won't be staying around."

In a way it made me feel good to hear that, but it made me feel bad, too. "Yeah," I mumbled through the numbness. "I was all set to leave when this tooth went crazy."

"Where are you headed?"

"San Francisco. To see my father."

"San Francisco's a beautiful place. I go there whenever I get a chance, which isn't often enough."

He wrote out a prescription, told me not to eat anything for a couple of hours, and sent me out to the receptionist to pay my bill. That hurt almost as much as the toothache.

Naturally Loreen made something unchewable for dinner. The anesthetic had worn off, and my jaw throbbed all night. It's been raining all day today, and Bonnie and Billy have been cooped up inside, fighting above the noise of the television. I really have to get out of here.

I didn't say anything to Grandma, but I didn't need to. She could sense that something is up. "The scrapbooks,

Dennis," she whispered. "Will you take them with you? Give them to your mother when you get back to Pennsylvania. That one'll get rid of them if you don't," she said, nodding toward the kitchen where Loreen was listening to a religious radio program.

"I will," I said, and made room for one carton in the back of my car.

I know she doesn't want me to go, and I hate to leave her here with nobody but Loreen and Tom and their nasty kids for company. Uncle Tom is a certified wonk who lets Loreen say whatever she wants to. It must be awful to get old and not be able to take care of yourself anymore and know that you're not wanted.

Tonight at supper I announced to the family that I am leaving tomorrow. We had canned spaghetti, french fries, and Nilla wafers. At least I could chew it. Grant would have a fit eating with this family. Even my mother, who believes that food should taste good and never mind the calories, would not have liked Loreen's idea of a dinner. I always thought farmers were healthy because they have gardens with all kinds of fresh stuff, but not here, not in Loreen's kitchen. I couldn't imagine that I'd ever actually *miss* vegetables, but I did in that house.

Grandma hardly touched her dinner, and I knew it was because she was sad that I was leaving, not just because of the bad food. I helped Loreen clean up the dishes, and then Grandma and I took a slow, stiff walk up to the hardtop road and back.

She said, "I've been wrong about a lot of things, Dennis. I'm real sorry."

I said, "That's okay. Everybody makes mistakes."

Oh boy, do they ever. Especially me.

Tape 11

Sunday, July 20th, Colorado.

What a day.

I got up early this morning and had my tent packed up and everything all set to go before the rest of the family was around. Darned if Loreen didn't show up, tying on an old brown bathrobe that looked as though it might belong to Uncle Tom, and offered to fix my breakfast. Maybe this was just because she was glad to see me leave, but it was a nice gesture and made me remember her a little more kindly.

She stirred water into a mix and made a huge stack of pancakes and set that in front of me with a bottle of syrup. While I ate she packed me a lunch, without asking what I wanted, and I didn't find out until a couple of hours later what it was.

I checked around to make sure I hadn't left anything behind. By then everybody was up. The kids came out, glared at me, said, "'Bye, Dennis," and ran off. Loreen said, "Good luck, Dennis." Uncle Tom said, "Say hello to your

mom when you see her." I wondered when that would be.
Then I went into Grandma's room. She was huddled under
the blankets just the way she was the first time I saw her.
I could tell she was crying. I couldn't make myself say good-
bye, so I hugged her and left.

It's beginning to feel as though I'm always leaving. My
feelings about leaving are always mixed. When I left the
Burg I was running away from Dr. Grant and his anger,
but it just about killed me to leave Stephanie. When I got
to Chicago there were Eugenia and Roxanne. Leaving them
was hard, too. I learned a lot from Eugenia, and it was
much different from the things I learned from Grandma.
Grandma was hard to leave, too, in a different way. She
needs me, and there isn't any way I can help her. I'm afraid
if somebody doesn't help her soon she'll die, just because
there isn't anything else to do. And she knows that too.

I followed Route 25 back up to I-80 and headed west
again. Mary Plymouth felt in good shape, ready to go some
miles. Unfortunately I was not watching the speedometer,
until I saw those blinking lights in my rearview mirror.
Then I checked the speedometer and it was at 67—no
chance he was after somebody else. I eased off the highway
onto the shoulder. The trooper parked behind me and came
up to stand by my car, peering in at me. He wore dark
glasses and I couldn't see his eyes. I handed him my license
and the registration; he nodded and walked back to his
cruiser, still not saying anything. Probably called head-
quarters to see if I stole the car. Probably thought I was
smuggling dope. I have heard that troopers sometimes

practically take your car apart if you're a kid and they think you might have drugs with you. My hands were sweating from nervousness while I waited, and I probably looked guilty.

He was standing next to me again. "Where are you going, Mr. Brown?"

"San Francisco," I told him. "Actually Berkeley. To see my father," I said. I don't know why I told him that. I tend to talk too much when I'm nervous.

"You in a big hurry?"

"Not really."

"Slow down then."

He wrote up a ticket and handed it to me with my license and registration. I was mad at myself. Again. I swore that from now on I will not go over 55. I really am not in a big hurry, but my money is running low.

Just past Ogallala I had to make a decision. I could continue on I-80 straight to San Francisco, cutting through a corner of Wyoming, or I could take I-70 instead and drive across Colorado and southern Utah. I was not sure until the last possible second which I would do, but then I decided on Colorado. I always wanted to see Colorado. Up ahead were the mountains looming at the edge of the flatness. Imagine how the early pioneers must have felt, coming across the plains in their covered wagons, not realizing what lay ahead of them. But then, neither did I.

I didn't stop in Denver. It's too easy to get lost in a big city; I'll save Denver for some other time. I kept going,

tell me.
id. "You

er Tang.
without

comes
middle
ke you

aiting

hand.

out

ide
ier
u

g,

suburban shopping center to
headed into the mountains.

ies, but as I was crossing the
ing that all the rivers west of
he Pacific instead of east—I
ry's temperature gauge and saw
blow. I pulled off the road and
od. Steam was coming out from
ld hear the water boiling. I know
take the cap off, because scalding
er you. You also don't pour in any
me time or you will crack the block.
, but then usually there is a lot going
. I sat under a tree and waited for Mary
pose it was the altitude, plus the strain
ing uphill, plus the fact that life is not
ght to. I wished I hadn't eaten up all of
es—ten slices of white bread with a little
holding pairs of them together.

g of a thick juicy burger dripping with
and ketchup when a pickup truck rolled
. A girl got out and walked toward me. She
n as a cowboy and she wore a white cowboy
eans. "You in trouble?" she asked.
ngine overheated."
d over to Mary and peered under the hood.
g to have to add some water when she cools

"I know that," I said. I didn't need this girl t

"I could give you a lift to a gas station," she s
got something to carry water in?"

All I had was a mayonnaise jar with some leftov

"You shouldn't drive through these mountains
extra water. How far you going?"

"San Francisco."

She shook her head. "Listen, after the mountain
the desert. Always carry plenty of water. Here it is,
of summer, and you got no water. Come on, I'll ta
someplace."

She jumped back in the cab of her truck without w
for an answer. I locked up Mary and followed her.

"Name's Texas McCoy," she said, sticking out her

"Dennis Brown," I said, shaking it.

"You drive all the way from Pennsylvania?"

"Yeah. Been visiting family."

"I'm from New Mexico," she said. "Up here to check
a stallion. Might be doing some trading."

"You have horses?"

"Yes, sir!" she said proudly. "The Lazy B Ranch outs
of Santa Fe. One of the best in the state." I looked at
hard. She didn't seem to be much older than I am. "Y
know anything about horses?" she asked.

"Not a thing. Always thought it would be interestin
though."

"Don't they have horses in Pennsylvania?"

"Yes, but I still don't know anything about them."

"I always wanted to go to Philadelphia," she said. "T

see the Liberty Bell and Independence Hall. You been to
Philadelphia?"

"No, never been there."

"You in school or working or what?"

"I just got out of high school. I'm going out to San
Francisco to visit my father."

She drove to a gas station off the main highway and I
bought a big plastic container for water, and I bought her a
burger because she was being so nice, and then because I
was hungry I had a burger, too, and because we were both
still hungry we split a third one. By the time we got back
to Mary the engine was cool enough to pour in the water.

All this time we were talking. She told me about her
grandfather, Pappy Ben, who left her a ranch with nothing
but debts, and how she had turned the whole thing around
practically by herself. And I told her about Eugenia Brown
and Grace Sunderland, and that opened up the whole box
of who my father is.

"I haven't seen my father in years," she said. "He's fishing in Alaska, last I heard. Tell you the truth, I don't care.
I can't imagine driving all the way across the country to find
a man who has not done one reasonable thing for you."

"It's important to me."

"Guess it is, or you wouldn't be doing it."

I didn't tell her about Stephanie, but I couldn't see that
that made any difference.

"Can I ask you something?" she asked.

"Sure."

"What's it like, being, uh, black?"

Nervy girl, this Texas. I don't think anybody ever actually asked me the question before. But it didn't seem like being nosy, more like asking for the sake of wanting to *know*.

"I don't think it's any different from being white, until somebody starts treating you different, if you understand what I mean. My little cousins, Bonnie and Billy, you could tell they were thinking of all the nasty things they had ever heard about niggers and they were just dying to say them to me, to see what I'd do. And back home, when I'd go out with girls, their parents would sooner or later get in an uproar about them going out with a *black* boy. That's when you know you're different, you're black, and the world treats you in a way that's different from the way it treats whites."

"Interesting," she said, and I could tell she was thinking about it hard. "You don't mind that I asked?"

"Of course I don't mind. Now can I ask you something?"

"Fair enough."

"What's it like being a cowgirl? I've never been around a girl who runs her own ranch and knows how to fix cars and do all the stuff you seem to know how to do."

She hesitated, and then she asked me, flat out, "You got a girlfriend?"

I stalled for a couple of seconds and worked at a dribble of ketchup that had fallen on my shirt.

"Yeah. I did when I left, anyway. I guess I still do."

"What's she like?"

"Look, you're supposed to be answering this question, not asking me more. I already answered one of yours."

"I can't answer you unless I know that," she said.

"She's a dancer," I said. "She's tall and thin like you, and she's in good shape, like you, but her work is dancing."

"Pretty?"

"Very."

"Do you think I'm pretty?"

I was getting *real* uncomfortable with the direction all this was taking. So I stalled again.

"Answer me. Do you think I'm pretty?"

"I think you're good-looking."

"Good-looking as she is?"

"Not the same way Stephanie is."

"That's what it feels like to be a cowgirl," she said, as though she had won an argument. "To have guys look at you and know that if you can run a ranch, you can do a lot of other things, too, maybe things that guys can't. They don't even think about whether you're pretty or not. Sometimes it matters, sometimes it doesn't. It's probably a lot like being black, or, in your case, not quite black. Most of the time I'm glad I'm who I am, that I can do the things I do, and that I look like what I am. But sometimes I'd like to be a pretty dancer. I can't change that any more than you can change the color of your skin."

I took another look at Texas. She had shoved her cowboy hat back on her head. Her hands were hard, like a man's, but her face wasn't. She looked soft and warm in the late afternoon sunlight, and I leaned over and kissed her. "I always wanted to kiss a cowgirl," I said.

She grinned. "Am I supposed to say I always wanted to kiss a black guy?"

It was Texas's idea that we pool our resources and find a place to camp. She didn't know much more about this area than I did, but she didn't seem to mind asking questions. She is one of these independent, take-charge kind of girls that you hear about, but I had never met one quite like her before. It was interesting, but—well, I don't know.

I needed somebody to talk to, somebody my own age who knew about the world. I hadn't been with anybody like that since I left home, and I've been gone for more than three weeks now.

I followed Texas back to the gas station. She picked up a map and some directions. "You okay on gas?" she asked. "This place we're going to is pretty far out in the country." I said I was. "Food and water? This is not one of those places that sells Mars Bars and Grape-Ade if you forget yours." I refilled the plastic jug with water while she was inside, and I had the box of groceries I bought back in Denver—enough to get me to California, according to my plan.

"Follow me," she said. You don't argue with a girl like Texas.

I was lost in a cloud of dust as we tore over a forest road. The road got rougher and rougher, and Mary struggled hard to keep up. I was scared that Mary would bottom out and do herself some permanent injury.

After miles of this we got to a lake with tall evergreens around it. Nothing fancy—pit toilets, no showers, no nothing, just lots of fresh mountain air and pine trees and beautiful scenery no matter which way you looked. Definitely worth the trip.

"What do you think, Dennis? Got anything like this back East?"

I had to admit I had never seen anything like it. "Looks good to me," I said. "Where are we going to put the tents?" I thought I was being polite, letting her have the say.

She looked at me scornfully. "What do you want a tent for? Nothing better than sleeping out under the stars. Afraid a bear is going to get you?"

"Bear?"

"Just kidding, Dennis. But it does happen sometimes."

This did not put my mind at ease. I thought it would be a good idea to put up the tent anyway, in case it rained or something, although it was as clear as could be. But it seemed like a very unmacho thing to do; better to go along with whatever Texas thought. After all, she's had a lot more experience in this part of the country than I have.

We had the place to ourselves. It was so far out that there was no ranger or anybody around. We decided to collect firewood, old branches and pine cones, so we could have a campfire after the sun went down. We didn't talk much while we worked. Texas got an ax out of her truck and started whacking the dead wood into short pieces. There was already a ring of blackened stones, and she stacked our firewood next to that. A good thing we brought our own drinking water, because there was none—just water from the lake.

We had gotten things nicely set up when we heard a motor, and pretty soon a pickup with a camper shell appeared on the other side of the lake.

"Company," Texas said. "Damn. I hope they stay over there."

But the motor kept on coming. It stopped not far from our campsite. Doors slammed and voices echoed out over the lake. They weren't more than fifty yards away, beyond some dense bushes.

"Okies," Texas said, sounding annoyed.

"Okies?"

"Oklahomans."

"You don't like people from Oklahoma?"

"Some are okay, some aren't. Like folks everywhere. Isn't it the same in Pennsylvania?"

"I guess so."

"We get lots of tourists around Santa Fe," she said. "They can get under your skin. Somehow when people go visiting some other place, they don't act right. I've heard that about a lot of people. Easterners aren't real popular where I come from, far as that goes."

"What's wrong with Easterners?"

"Probably nothing, as long as they stay in the East. They're kind of loud, if you know what I mean. Aggressive."

"Am I loud and aggressive?"

"No, but you're different."

"You know what I think, Texas? I think you're prejudiced."

But before we could get into a debate about that, our attention was caught by the new arrivals. We could hear every word they said. One was complaining about not being able to find any water, and someone else said he had seen a couple of people over yonder, which was us, and he'd go over and see if they knew where they could get water.

"Here they come," Texas muttered.

A big, red-faced, beefy man with his beer belly hanging over his belt came crashing through the bushes like a rhinoceros.

"Howdy, folks," he said.

"Howdy," said Texas, and I said "Howdy," too, feeling silly.

"Mighty nice place here," he said, and we went on like that for a minute or two, but meanwhile he was sizing us up. Especially me. "You kids know where we can get some drinking water? Didn't know we was supposed to bring our own."

"I can give you some," Texas said, "but we don't have much to spare ourselves." She went over to her truck and lifted out her plastic jug. "You got something to put it in?"

"I'll go get something." The whole time her back was turned, this joker was staring right at me. He spit on the ground, stared some more, and went back through the bushes.

"I don't like that guy," I whispered to Texas.

"Yeah, he looks like kind of a mean one," she said, but not too seriously.

"No, I mean it. I think he's dangerous."

"Oh, come on, Dennis. What's wrong with you? He's just a stupid redneck."

"Texas, he looked at you and he looked at me and he doesn't like the two of us together."

"You're letting your imagination go crazy," she said. "You expecting him to come back with a shotgun and run us off?"

"I don't know. I just don't like it."

Pretty soon the guy came crashing through again with a small jug. There was another guy with him. Same type. Tiny blue eyes. They both wore caps with bills with COORS across the front. They each carried a can of beer, and I figured they had been popping beers for a couple of hours. They set down two unopened cans on a flat stone. "That there's in trade for the drinking water."

"Thanks, but it's not necessary. Neither of us drink." I said that not knowing if it was true for Texas, but it didn't matter. I didn't want to accept anything from them. I wanted them to go away.

They stood around, swallowing their beer, in no hurry to take their water and leave. "Long as you're not going to drink them," the second one said, flipping open one of the gift beers. He spilled some on his shirt.

"I see one of you's from Pennsylvania and the other one's from New Mexico," said the first guy.

"That's right."

"Which one's from Pennsylvania?"

"I am."

He walked closer, right up to me. I could see the blood vessels in his bleary little eyes. "We don't like it much when black boys from the East come out here and mess around with our white girls," he said.

What was I supposed to say or do with that one? My mind spun and came up blank. It's hard to think straight when you're that mad. I didn't move, and I didn't answer.

"You hear what I said, *boy?*"

His belly was almost touching me. I never wanted to hit anybody so much in my life, not since the kid in first grade. But I knew if I did, the two of them would pound me to jelly. Big and fat and probably out of shape, but I couldn't take them both on.

"All right, you bastards, back off."

It was Texas. She had a .22 rifle in her hands, and it was pointed at the guy with the water jug. They spun around and stared at her, mouths hanging open.

"Well, now, say there, little lady, why don't you just put that gun down, there's a good girl." The slobbery one started walking toward her.

"Don't move another inch," she said.

The guy took a step, as though he thought she was bluffing. She fired one shot into his plastic jug. Water squirted everywhere. He stopped in his tracks. "Hey now, listen *here.*"

"Dennis, get in your car and start driving," Texas said softly. "You two, stay right where you are. Put your hands up and don't move."

"What are you going to do?"

"I'm coming, don't worry. I'm not going to stay here with these farts, believe me. Now *go*."

I dived into my car. Thank God she started right up. I worried about being chased twelve miles back to town by those maniacs, over that awful road. But Texas had her rifle pointed out the window of the pickup with her left hand. I didn't doubt for a second that she could fire as well with her left as she did with her right. The two bozos were still standing there with their hands in the air. She spun the pickup around to follow me, and as she did I saw the two guys running through the bushes toward their camper. I heard a shot. I didn't want to find out who fired. I gunned Mary down the bumpy road fast as she could take it with Texas roaring along right behind me.

We boiled dust for several miles, until the road widened. Texas flashed her lights and I pulled over. She was grinning from ear to ear. "Didn't realize life was so exciting out here, did you?"

"I don't need this kind of excitement. What was that shot?"

"Me. I blew out their tire. That'll slow them down for a while and give us a chance to clear out."

"Isn't that against the law?"

"Sure. But so's what they were going to do to you."

I didn't want to think about that. "My sleeping bag is still back there. And so's your ax."

"I got the ax. Sorry about your sleeping bag. I didn't see it. Stop when we get back into town and we'll talk about what we're going to do next."

By the time we reached town it was dark, and we had both done some thinking. "You'd better keep going," Texas said.

"What about you?"

"I'll be okay. But it isn't a good idea for us to be seen together. People notice things like that, don't they?"

"Yeah. Listen, have you ever read *Othello*?"

"No. Who's that?"

"A character in a play. Listen, Texas, maybe I'll come and see you someday."

"You'd be welcome," she said and shook my hand. Then she climbed into her truck and drove away. And I'm going west again.

I wondered where she'd go and what she'd do. She didn't seem scared—just mad. Texas is an unusual girl. I don't think I ever met anybody like her. But I'd like to again. Life wouldn't be dull.

Tape 12

Monday, July 21st, Nevada someplace.

I stayed last night near a town called Rifle. Probably a good name, under the circumstances. It had a little campground. I was too nervous to set up my tent, and my sleeping bag is back with the Oklahomans. I was glad to get away with my skin. My _black_ skin, which is what caused the problem.

So I spent last night in the car, not sleeping much, on the off-chance that the bozos might have decided to check out all campgrounds as far as the Utah border. The Pennsylvania plates are a dead giveaway, no matter where I am. I haven't seen many Pennsylvania licenses west of the Mississippi.

I have a lot on my mind. Is this the way people react to interracial couples? Mother tried to tell me that life outside the Burg is different. The reactions back there were fairly subtle, just a few parents who didn't want their daughters going out with me and lied about the reason.

But when I did go out with white girls, to the movies or school dances or McDonald's, nobody got ugly or violent.

I wonder if anything like this happened to my mother and father when they were together. "We never went to the South," she said. "It was bad enough in the North."

Scrunched up under the steering wheel, trying to find a comfortable position to catch a nap but still alert to anybody who might be snooping around, I kept thinking about my mother. She tried to protect me from the kind of thing that had just happened. But you can't protect somebody by keeping them away from bad situations. I think it's better if you teach them how to take care of themselves. Texas is a good example of somebody who knows how to take care of herself.

This got me to thinking about the women I know. I never realized before that my life is full of women. First my mother. Then Stephanie. Two grandmothers, who could not be more different from each other. Roxanne, who complicated my life. And now Texas McCoy, a whole new breed. My brain went round and round until the sky started brightening. The daylight made me feel safe enough to catch a couple of hours of sleep.

It was eight o'clock when I finally crawled out of that miserable front seat and found a water pump so I could wash my face. I felt filthy. There is a certain kind of smell you get when you've been scared and sweating from fear, and I wanted to wash that smell away. The small lake had a sign saying NO SWIMMING. There were people fishing.

If I had had a fishing rod I would have tried my luck. I strolled around until I found a kind of inlet that was out of view of most people, and then I "fell in." The water was so cold it took my breath away. I didn't have any soap with me, but I scrubbed at my skin with a handful of leaves until I felt clean.

I was really hungry. Starving, in fact. That's when I remembered my box of groceries was back there with the sleeping bag. I scrounged around in the backseat and found a jar of dry-roasted peanuts, pretty stale, but I ate them all. That kept me going as far as Grand Junction, only a few miles from the state line. I wanted to get out of Colorado and into Utah, not exactly the promised land, but at least out of a state where somebody might be looking for me.

I bought a loaf of bread and a jar of peanut butter and studied the map. Arches National Park was not far away, and I went there. I wished I had a camera. I didn't expect Utah to be so beautiful. I'm not a photography bug, but it was so spectacular that I wanted to capture it and save it. Instead I bought postcards for all the women I've been thinking about.

There was a patch of shade near the visitors' center, where I sat to write my postcards. First I addressed them all. Then I couldn't think what to say to anybody. That's why I hate to write letters, because I can't think of what I want to say when I'm sitting there with a pen in my hand, even though when I'm walking down the street or driving along the highway my head is full of all the things I'd say if that person was there.

I put the postcards in my pocket and hiked back to Landscape Arch, which has a span of 291 feet and a height of 105 feet, one of the biggest natural stone arches in the world. It was a mile from the road and very hot. Then I got back on the road again.

Interstate 70 came to an end, and I picked up another highway that headed west. I stopped for gas in a town named Delta and started across the desert, thinking about Moses and all those Bible people. I saw a lot of desert before I got to Nevada.

Now I'm in Nevada, which is the most peculiar place imaginable. It looks like the moon out here, miles and miles of barrenness. Once in awhile there's a town, some desolate place where it seems nothing in the world could ever happen, and I wonder how anybody can stand to live there. I feel sad and lonely, just driving down the main street. Suppose my car breaks down here and for some reason I have to *stay* here for the rest of my life, in Nevada, in some tiny town miles from the next tiny town.

I found a place near Ely to put my tent, and I made a bed out of a pile of clothes. It's hot and dusty, and this place doesn't have any showers either, or a lake to jump into legally or illegally. But there is a water pump, and I stuck my head under it and let it wash all over me. I'm so tired I can't think.

Tuesday, July 22nd, Sacramento, California. On Pacific Time and almost there.

I was glad to leave Nevada. One of the things I noticed

is the slot machines all over the place, even in the diners. I had never seen one before. I wanted to play it, but you have to be twenty-one. So I watched somebody else feed it quarters and pull the lever. Nothing happened. I was thinking I had saved myself a bunch of money when this old guy with a weatherbeaten face hit the jackpot and a whole river of quarters came gushing out. He counted them and started feeding them back in again.

I poked along slowly, stopping in a little town called Eureka, population 600, where I got some coffee.

"They call this the loneliest road in America," the waitress said. I was the only customer in the diner. "Said it right in *Time* magazine. I got a letter of apology from the American Automobile Association, for making that remark." She had the letter framed and hanging next to the cash register. "Suits me fine, though. I like it this way."

I'll be in San Francisco tomorrow, and that means I'll soon be seeing my father. I keep telling myself this is the reason I've come all this way—to find out who he is so I can start to find out who *I* am. And that scares me.

My plan, which I developed since I left Nebraska, was to check into a motel before I get to San Francisco, shower, and get myself all cleaned up. Make sure my fingernails are clipped. Find a Laundromat and wash all my clothes. Maybe clean out my car and wash it. I had thought I might even buy a new pair of jeans and a shirt and maybe new sneakers, but now that's out of the question. I can't afford anything new.

And then my plan was to call my father and tell him I'm

coming to see him. This is where the plan ends. I'm not sure where I can find him, or what I'll say on the phone or what I'll do when I see him. And I am getting more and more nervous about the whole thing.

I've run the scene through my head several different ways. In one version I call, my dad answers the phone, I tell him who I am, and he gets excited and tells me to come right over; I go and he hugs me and it's as if we've never been apart.

In the second version I don't call, I go straight to his place; he comes to the door and says, "Yes?" because he doesn't recognize me. I tell him who I am. Then there are two possibilities: A, he hugs me and it is as if we have never been apart, or, B, he is very polite but makes it clear that he wants no part of me. In ending B I am disappointed, but I understand. He has put together another life without me. We shake hands and agree to keep in touch from time to time. It's not the answer I want, but at least it's an answer. I'm not heartbroken, because I don't like him very much anyway.

All the way across Nevada, that's what I thought about. Somewhere outside of Sacramento I was too tired to go any farther, and I found a cheap motel and parted with a few of the small handful of dollars I have left. Fortunately I had transferred the last of my cash to my wallet, out of my sleeping bag, which was now on some godforsaken mountain in Colorado, or maybe incinerated by some enraged Oklahomans.

I took a hot shower and asked at the desk for directions

to a Laundromat. I washed everything except what I was wearing and dried it and changed into clean clothes in the bathroom and ran the clothes I had just taken off through another machine. I decided to save the quarter for the drier and hang up those few things in the motel bathroom.

I bought a cheap razor and scraped off the fuzz. Maybe I can get a haircut somewhere. I smoothed out the dry clothes and tried to fold them neatly so they wouldn't look so wrinkled. I checked my dad's 1960s suit for spots and decided it still looked okay.

The motel is the cheap kind with no television unless you pay extra. I decided to pay extra, to treat myself well this last night on the road, and to buy a fried chicken dinner and eat it in my room while I watched TV. When I went out to get the chicken I found a pay phone and called the number copied from my mother's address book. As I punched in the number, my mouth went dry and my hands started to sweat, and I tried to remember what it was I was going to say to him when he answered.

No answer. Maybe he was at work. After I ate and watched some TV I went out to the pay phone and tried again.

Still no answer. If he plays piano somewhere, then he's probably there and won't be home until one o'clock in the morning, at least, and I might as well forget it until tomorrow.

Just in case, I tried again a few minutes ago. It's almost midnight. No answer.

* * *

Now I know. And nothing has turned out the way I expected.

When I woke up this morning, I knew that if he worked late he was still probably asleep and it would not be a good idea to wake him up. I drove for a while and stopped to call again about ten. I must have missed him. He'd gone out somewhere.

I put on his suit and one of his shirts and drove to Berkeley, across the bay from San Francisco. I didn't know what to do next. I got off the interstate and pulled into a gas station and tried to find someone who knew where this address is. Nobody did. Then a highway patrolman stopped. He was such a nice guy, he said he'd lead me there. "It's not that far away," he said. I told him it's my father. He had noticed my Pennsylvania plates and said, "He's going to be real happy to see you."

I followed the cop, who cruised slowly down a narrow street, stopped, and pointed. It was the right street and house number. He waved and made a circle with his thumb and finger for luck and drove off. I had to hunt for a place to park. Then I was so nervous I could hardly maneuver the car into it.

It is a row house, neat, in a neighborhood of small houses with a few trees on the street. There are flowers in a tiny patch of dirt by the steps and flowers in a windowbox up above, bright red ones mixed with white and purple. Petunias, I think.

I went into an entryway. There was a row of buttons with names beside them. I found it easily: J. D. Brown—

2A. I rang the bell next to the name, hardly breathing. Then a buzzer sounded, and it sank in too late that I was supposed to push open the inside door. A woman was coming out, and she let me in. I climbed a flight of stairs. One apartment door toward the back had a B on it. I walked toward the front. My knees were shaking. I found A. This would be the one with the red and white and purple petunias. I rang the doorbell and wiped my wet hands on my pants.

I could hear someone inside, footsteps, a lock being taken off, *click click*. A man opened the door. He looked half asleep. He had on khakis sagging without a belt, a T-shirt, and bare feet. He needed a shave and his hair was standing on end.

The man was white.

"Yes?" he said.

My tongue stuck to the roof of my mouth. "I'm looking for James Brown," I managed to say.

"He's not here. Who are you?" He talked in a grumble.

"I'm Dennis Brown. I'm his son."

"Jamie's son? I didn't even know he had a son."

That hit me in the gut. "Where is he? Is he here?" Voice shaking, knees wobbling.

The man scratched his stomach under his T-shirt. "He's in Houston. Left about two weeks ago. He's got a gig there. Won't be back until sometime in September. Did he know you were coming?"

"No," I said, trying not to cry.

"Look, what did you say your name is? Dennis? Come on in."

He stepped back and made room for me, and I stumbled past him.

"My name is Pete," he said, sticking out his hand. "I'm just crashing here while Jamie's in Houston. There's plenty of room for you, too, if you were planning to stay here."

It's a nice apartment. Simple but nice. Very plain, but lots of light. Not much furniture, except for a beautiful grand piano that takes up most of the room. Mats on the floor. Except for that piano, it could be a cell for a Buddhist monk, although I don't know much about monks of any kind. I went over and touched the keyboard so Pete wouldn't see I was ready to bawl.

"You play?" Pete asked.

"I fool around a little. Are you a musician?"

"Yeah. Clarinet. Jamie and I work together sometimes. Look, why don't I make some coffee for us both, and then I'll go get myself together and you can sort of relax, lay back, get *your*self together. Okay?"

He went behind a screen to a tiny kitchen area and ran water into a kettle. "When it boils, just pour some water through the filter," he said and disappeared into the bathroom.

I tried to think. My father isn't here, and that's that. I don't have enough money to go to Houston or anywhere else.

There's about eleven dollars left in my pocket, including

change. The only thing I have that's worth any money is my tape deck. That and my car. If I sold them I could stay here and get a job until my father gets back. Or I could buy a bus ticket to the Burg. Get my old job back with Gochy. Find a way to see Stephanie.

Stephanie seems like a dream, as much of a dream as my father. If I concentrate I can picture her face, her beautiful body in her dancer's leotard, her hands with the long, thin fingers. I can feel her skin, smell her hair right after she's washed it.

She told me to go figure out what I want to do with my life.

If I go back now, I still won't know. It would be back to the same old thing, and I don't want the same old thing anymore. I've learned too much, but I'm still scared of what's out there ahead of me. I want my father to tell me, but he isn't here. I'm going to have to figure it out for myself.

The kettle whistled. I poured boiling water through the coffee in the filter, enough to make two cups. I found a mug in the sink and carried it over to the piano. I took a few sips and set it on the windowsill.

I sat down at my father's piano. The wood gleamed in the sun streaming through the window. Music is stacked in piles in an old bookcase. I played a few chords and tested a couple of progressions, trying to recall some of the theory that Eugenia talked about.

Then I remembered Paul Robeson's voice: "Deep, deep river . . . my home is over Jordan." I took the melody in the bass, thinking about poor old Moses, wandering all those years in the wilderness. I'm wandering in the wilderness, too. I hope I don't have to stay here for forty years. Another spiritual. My fingers moved easily over the keys. I didn't have to tell them what to do.

When I stopped for another swallow of coffee, Pete had come back and was watching me. His hair was slicked back and he had on pressed jeans and a plaid shirt. I felt very self-conscious in my father's antique suit. I probably looked pretty strange.

"Incredible," Pete said. "For a minute there I could have sworn it was Jamie. You look a lot like him. You even *sound* like him. Incredible."

"I do?"

"The way you sit at the piano, exactly the way he does. And you *coax* out the music. That's the way he does it. You a musician, too?"

I didn't even have to think about it. "Yes," I said. "I'm planning to be."

Suddenly everything clicked into place. I have no idea how I am going to do it. There's an awful lot to learn, a lot of catching up to do. It doesn't matter. In that minute I knew where I am going. I know what the Promised Land is going to be. "Can I use your phone?"

I called my mother, collect. "The West residence." I let the operator get past Corky to Mother. She was really excited. "Oh, Denny, I'm so glad to hear your voice! How are you?" she sang out, over a few thousand miles of telephone line.

"Great, Mother," I said.

"Where are you?"

"I'm at Dad's, in Berkeley. Only he isn't here—he's in Houston, and he won't be back for a couple of months."

I told her I am going to stay and that I want to study music. Maybe this is the place to be; maybe it isn't. *Where* isn't important any more. I know where I'm going, who I am, who I want to be. She started to argue and then stopped. I guese she knew it was okay.

"Somebody wants to say hello," she said finally.

Stephanie came on the line. She was crying. It was so good to hear her voice I almost cried, too. She told me she loved me, and I told her I loved her.

"I'm leaving next week," she said." Mother wants me to go to Maine with her for the month of August. I'll finish high school in Philadelphia. Then I don't know what's going to happen. My parents don't want me to be a dancer."

"Why not?"

"Long story, Denny They say dancing is a wonderful discipline but an 'unnatural' life. When are you coming home?"

"I don't know." The connection was terrible. "I'm going to study music, Stephanie," I shouted at her. "I don't know how or where, but that's what I want."

"That's wonderful, Denny!" she yelled back. "But when will we ever see each other again?" It sounded like a wail.

"I don't know. But we will, I promise you that. Just remember—Philadelphia!"

"Philadelphia!"

I hung up. It was okay now to cry.

Tomorrow I'll pack away my tapes, sell my tape recorder, and go look for a job.

This is Dennis Brown signing off, Wednesday, July 23rd, Berkeley, California.

Carolyn Meyer grew up in rural Pennsylvania, where she made up her mind at the age of six to be a writer. In the years that followed she majored in English in college, worked at a couple of boring jobs, brought up three sons—and wrote. She has lived in New Mexico since 1978 and has traveled widely, learning about people and their cultures, from the Eskimos of Alaska to the Maya of Yucatan, from South Africa to Japan. She is married to the poet and historian, E. A. Mares. This is her twenty-seventh book.